The Secret of the Three Bullets

How New Nuclear Weapons Are Back on the Battlefield

Maurizio Torrealta
and
Emilio Del Giudice

Published by:
Trine Day LLC
PO Box 577
Walterville, OR 97489
1-800-556-2012
www.TrineDay.com
publisher@TrineDay.net

Library of Congress Control Number: 2014947479

Torrealta, Maurizio and Del Giudice, Emilio.
The Secret of the Three Bullets–1st ed.
p. cm.
Epub (ISBN-13) 978-1-937584-27-6
Mobi (ISBN-13) 978-1-937584-28-3
Print (ISBN-13)978-1-937584-26-9
1. Fiction. 2. Nuclear Weapons--Mini. 3. Cold Fusion. I. Torrealta,
Maurizio and Del Giudice, Emilio. Y. II. Title

First Edition
10 9 8 7 6 5 4 3 2 1

Printed in the USA
Distribution to the Trade by:
Independent Publishers Group (IPG)
814 North Franklin Street
Chicago, Illinois 60610
312.337.0747
www.ipgbook.com

INTRODUCTION

In our investigations up till now, we have reported stories that are terrible but true, and yet they have had no apparent effect. So here we will tell the same stories as though they were the fruit of our imagination, hoping in this way to stimulate the reader's fantasy – something that we have absolutely refrained from doing in our previous work – thus enriching their perception of these dramatic events which are occurring in absolute silence, or have already occurred and been totally ignored. It is this lack of perception, this slumbering of intelligence that most concerns us, and for which we feel partially responsible, since we work in the news sector. So, with the stumbling gait of those who prefer to move rather than stand still and wait, we have created a fictional character as imperfect as we are, who we could only have called Claudio – from the Latin *claudicans* (*limping*) – a character created by superimposing four real people: Flaviano Masella, Mario Sanna, Angelo Saso and Maurizio Torrealta, strictly in alphabetical order. These four journalists are part of the *"Inchieste"* (Investigations) group from the Rainews24 television channel, and found themselves traveling around the world following a particular line of research.

Starting with a news report on the research carried out by a group of scientists from ENEA in Frascati on the theme of cold fusion, we then expanded our investigation, touching on England, South Lebanon and the United States, with the aim of finding answers to some simple questions: why was valid research into room-temperature fusion deliberately ignored? Why was enriched uranium found in a crater caused by a bomb in Khiam, Southern Lebanon? Why do depleted uranium bullets produce a temperature of 4000°C? Why are there traces of other radioactive elements in those bullets? How do the new bombs dropped on Gaza work, bombs that are able to amputate people's legs while leaving no trace of metal fragments? The answers to these questions are linked to one another by a secret that has been kept hidden for more than twenty years: the discovery of a process in physics that has enabled the production of nuclear bombs the size of a bullet, probably already used in the main theaters of war in the recent past and the immediate present. A secret that is intricately linked to the famous "Groves Memorandum," a document withheld until 1975, in which James B. Conant, president of the National Defense Research Council[1] and for many years also President of Harvard university, suggested to officials in the American administration that "dirty" uranium be used to pollute enemy cities with clouds of radioactive nanoparticles, accurately foreseeing its effects on the health of the people involved, effects that became a reality in Iraq, Kosovo, Afghanistan and the Lebanon: in other words, in the areas actually bombed with tons of dirty uranium by the so-called democratic countries.

Clearly, this is just a novel, loosely based on facts. Some names are fictional, but much of the evidence reported here was recorded during our investigations and, even though it may seem based on fantasy or totally absurd, it is in fact true. To allow our readers to feel the same surprise as we did when, during our investigations, we came across results that were simply unbelievable – in the literal sense of the word – we published in italics, the words in Claudio's reports that correspond to the witnesses' accounts that we recorded in the field. Often the truth is so unbelievable that it can be told as though it were a figment of the imagination. The story is strewn with historical information about people who really existed: Edward Teller, Alfred Coehn, Percy Williams Bridgman, James B. Conant, Martin Fleischmann, Stanley Pons and S.T. Cohen are all "historical figures" from the world of science, and often the world of war, too. Some of them have also become characters in our story: it is up to the reader to determine whether we are fantasizing or simply recounting what really happened.

When tackling complex issues like the one in this book, there is inevitably more than one truth. On the other hand, we authors do not belong to that genre of journalist that is always looking for a scoop, and we do not want to astound anyone by using special effects. It is up to the reader to decide whether this story is fantastic and unbelievable, imaginative but plausible, or improbable but true. We merely wish that the great gift which destiny has bestowed on human beings, the gift of being able to observe the world around us and speculate upon it, should once again become a fundamental legacy of the community.

Aware as we are of how fragile free thought can be, we nonetheless insist upon it, and still presumptuously attempt to reason on these topics which, on closer observation, can be understood simply by using the bases provided by our high school education, together with the arrogance implicit in asking questions which, in a free country like ours, is common to those frequenting cafés, reading newspapers or doing the housework with the radio constantly on. And when our knowledge proved to be inadequate – and this often happened – an extremely competent community of Italian scientists came to our rescue, generously devoting themselves to study and research.

This enormous human heritage – that is often unexploited, and sometimes actively "stolen" from our country – for which other countries continue to envy us, was the aspect that we were most pleased to discover in this whole work, and was also a source of invaluable assistance. Of all these unexpected guardian angels of knowledge, the one most selflessly close to us, who shared secrets, hypotheses and reasoning, as well as phone numbers and friends, was the theoretical physicist Emilio Del Giudice who, every time he speaks, offers us the precious illusion that we understand nuclear physics as well as we understand the layout of Rome. His role as co-author of this book is profoundly motivated by the wish to maintain the illusion of having understood nuclear physics. To retain the fictional aspect of the book, Emilio Del Giudice also appears in it as a character named Kurt Grass, in "homage" to his physical appearance.

As journalists and writers we cultivate a hope that the term "depleted uranium" is finally, and as soon as possible, replaced in journalistic reports by the term "dirty uranium" or "uranium charged with hydrogen isotopes" or at least that the term no longer appears without the adjective "so-called." There are terms like "limbo" or "celestial spheres" that have been canceled from theology works, or remain as mere evidence of temporary and false knowledge, as human beings' knowledge only can be. The same thing must occur with the term "depleted uranium," not because it does not exist, but because that uranium is not the one being used in battlefields. This change is increasingly necessary after the declassification of the "Groves Memorandum," more than thirty-four years ago. Henceforth, those who continue to use that expression will fully demonstrate their stubborn superficiality and ignorance.

A final recommendation to our readers: that they may at last learn to reject the adjectives associated with the names of the new weapons: "ecological nuclear," "sustainable atom-ic," "surgical nuclear," "virtual nuclear weapons," "deterrence factors," "robust earth penetrators," "technical deterrence," "deterrence effects," "nuclear building demolisher," and so on. Sooner or later, the countries that are guilty of using them will have to admit it.

So, let's hope that our readers will refuse these contra-dictions in terms, leaving them to the moral tightrope walkers, and learn to view these weapons for what they really are: tactical nuclear weapons. And above all, that they are aware of what this expression implies. Happy reading.

It was a period of patient work in the laboratory, of crucial experiments and daring action, of many false starts and many untenable conjectures. It was a time of earnest correspondence and hurried conferences, of debate, criticism, and brilliant mathematical improvisation....For those who participated, it was a time of creation; there was terror as well as exaltation in their new insight. It will probably not be recorded very completely as history. As history, its re-creation would call for an art as high as the story of Oedipus or the story of Cromwell, yet in a realm of action so remote from our common experience that it is unlikely to be known to any poet or any historian.

– Robert Oppenheimer

Chapter One

That Strange
Phone Call

The professor came out of the airport in San Francisco as though breathlessly surfacing from a long dive. He went over to a taxi.

"Can you take me to Union Square?"

The taxi turned onto US Route 101 North. The professor collapsed on the back seat and gazed out of the window, his eyebrows arching, wrinkles crinkling, eyes narrowing. Even the taxi driver could see it in his face.

What an awful journey: an hour waiting on the plane in Salt Lake City before take off, then missing the connecting flight to London and now looking for a hotel with his gut as heavy as lead.

The taxi raced along Bayshore. It was a summer evening in 1989. Out on the bay, a glimpse of bluish mist hanging over the water created a sight that would have soothed the most restless of spirits, but had not the slightest effect on the professor. The taxi stopped at Union Square, the victory monument towering over the center of the plaza. The taxi drove off and the professor walked towards one hotel, then decided on another. The distress of this unplanned night in San Francisco would have warranted the best downtown hotel, but for just a few hours, it made no difference where he stayed.

The professor walked up to the reception desk and mumbled, "I'd like a room for the night ...."

The telephone on the desk rang, interrupting him, and the man behind the counter quickly picked it up.

"Who? When did he arrive? Are you sure? Who's speaking? One moment, please ...."

Then, turning to the professor, "It's for you, sir. Professor Teller wants to talk to you."

The professor grabbed the phone.

"Who is this? Who's speaking?" Questions stuttered without even waiting for an answer. "Who? From where? I don't understand ... Who is this?"

On the other end of the line, a voice with a strong Hungarian accent answered.

"It's Professor Edward Teller. I heard you were going away to have an operation, so I'd like to wish you all the best for a speedy recovery. But I also wanted to take this opportunity to have some information about your experiment, the charge level and optimal electric field ... if I'm not disturbing you, of course."

The professor, with a barely visible movement of his lips, uttered polite trivialities followed by equally trivial technical suggestions.

"Proceed gradually with the charge. After a certain period, within a few weeks, heating will occur ... we're still in the experimental stage and have to advance with caution...."

But his face told a different story.

How the hell does he know where I am, if I didn't even know I was coming here? So they're following me. Why?

The call ended with mutual niceties.

"... let me know how it goes. We're all thinking of you."

"I'm happy you called. Thank you so much for your concern. See you soon."

He hung up the phone and asked to be taken to his room.

"Did you have a good trip?" asked the bellboy. "Shall I get you a drink from the bar? Do you want me to raise your room temperature?"

The professor did not answer, closed the door and even forgot to tip him. He threw himself onto the bed, closed his eyes and began to think.

Teller, the man who inspired the figure of Dr. Strangelove – the mad scientist who could not keep his arm from making the Nazi salute.[2] When he arrived in the US, he fought with all the scientists involved in the Manhattan Project. For him, Los Alamos was a den of Communists. He wanted to produce the H-bomb at all costs, even though not one of his calculations was correct … he got the military establishment to set up a laboratory just for him, because he couldn't get along with anyone else. He's an awesome person, a hugely intelligent man but entirely out of control and too close to the military. If someone had sent me an envelope containing five bullets, I'd feel better than I do now, receiving his best wishes for a speedy recovery. Recovery …. Right, but what's wrong with me?

So many tiny tumors in the colon caused by something that no one could explain.

Why did they delay the plane to organize this stupid farce of a phone call before I left for London? The message is clear: "You're being followed. Don't speak to anyone. We can find you whenever we want. Get lost, because the things you know must never be revealed."

I'm not so paranoid that I can be scared by a "good luck" phone call. But it's still a call from the father of the hot fusion bomb to the father of cold fusion, which already indicates a slight difference of opinion, if only for a question of temperature. If Teller had called me at home or at the university, that'd be fine … but in this hotel … my fears are definitely founded.

"When you know why you're afraid, you no longer fear," he said out loud.

The professor seemed heartened by this clarity, brightened up, took a packet of peanuts from the fridge, ate them and started thinking again.

Why is he having me followed? Everything I do has been made public now …. We talked about it all at the press conference, me and my colleague. There must be something about the research I'm doing or have already done that worries Teller. We both started as chemists. Like me, he did research into hydrogen. His thesis dealt with the first detailed treatment of the hydrogen molecular ion and I'm doing something similar. Perhaps he knows something I don't. Maybe he wants to use what I've discovered for purposes different from mine. One thing is sure: this is just the beginning, he won't stop, and it's certainly not a good start.

Chapter Two

THE SCIENTISTS INVOLVED IN ENEA'S REPORT 41

Florence, summer 2006.

Claudio leans forwards and murmurs into the ear of Norma, a blonde girl sitting in the row before his, "That's the eighth time he's said 'so to speak.'"

"Is it a conference on new wars, or a meeting of stammering militants?" she answers, without turning her head.

"He who knows, does not speak ... and he who speaks does not know. This man falls into the second category," he replied under his breath.

"And how do we meet the first, if those who know ... just keep quiet?"

It is hot, chaotic, in the lecture hall. This is not an ordinary lecture, even if there is a respectful silence before and after every speech. A man at the speakers' table announces a coffee break. Claudio jumps to his feet, trying to catch up with Norma and carry on the conversation, when an elderly gentleman, with a courtesy uncommon to those in the room, comes up to him and whispers in a low voice, "You must forgive me for disturbing you, my name is Professor Palazzi, I greatly appreciate the investigations that you and your group of journalists are conducting and, if I may, I would like to suggest a particular subject to you ..."

Claudio's eyes follow Norma as she walks away with a group of people and he sighs as he answers, "Tell me, Professor Palazzi."

"Cold fusion. On 23 March 1989, as you may recall, two professors from Salt Lake City announced that it was possible to produce low energy nuclear reactions. This announcement sparked ferocious debate: they were accused of falsifying data, superficiality and all possible scientific misconduct. Now a group of scientists from ENEA, the National Agency for Atomic and Alternative Energy in Italy, chaired by a renowned Nobel laureate, has verified that the experiment can be replicated and has also identified the reproducibility values. You might find it very interesting to look into. Get in touch with this theoretical physicist," he says, handing over a business card.

Then, with the same courtesy, he takes his leave. "I apologize if I have disturbed you and taken up your precious time. Thank you once again for what you are doing ..."

Claudio stands quite still, Norma now completely forgotten.

What he had been hoping for has finally happened: someone who knows and has not yet spoken, has very timidly handed him restricted information. And all of a sudden, his list of priorities changes: get back to the office, contact the ENEA group, study cold fusion, get further information on the scientists working on it. The business card ... he must not forget it, and he quickly writes the name and phone number in his diary.

The place is really strange: too impersonal to be called a village and too old-fashioned for a research center. But the chaos reigning there gives the impression that an irrepressible form of vitality continues to survive within that disorder. Dr. Garbati politely greets Claudio as she ushers him into an anonymous Seventies-style building. On the door of the laboratory, there is a strange symbol: FF11018.

"We worked in this workshop from 1999 to 2002. This is the constant temperature chamber that hosted the electrolysis experiment. We conducted an experiment in which it was possible to simultaneously measure excess heat and the eventual production of helium 4, which is the sign that the fusion event has a nuclear nature," the researcher tells him.

"What event?" asks Claudio.

"The cold fusion of two hydrogen nuclei or, if you prefer, of their isotope, deuterium."

Claudio smiles to himself, thinking that he has no idea what "deuterium" is, then asks, "Why don't you explain the whole story to me from the beginning?"

"In 1999, when the Nobel laureate became president of this institution, we witnessed a favorable sort of astral combination: we were given one billion, 150 million lire and a period of thirty-six months to verify, ten years after the announcement in Salt Lake City, whether cold fusion was a hoax or an amazing discovery. In April 2002 we sent a note to the president to inform him that we were ready to report on the project. The results we had obtained showed that the theory of cold fusion was valid: there was in fact a direct relationship between increase in the production of helium-four atoms and the production of heat.[3] The Nobel laureate was very happy with the news, and even joined us in drawing up a report, offering a great deal of advice and many suggestions.

"A few days later, however, the situation changed dramatically: the magazines, for various reasons, did not publish the report, the Nobel laureate could no longer be found, but no one said 'this can't be done' or 'this is wrong.' Everything stood still until the autumn of 2002 when we decided to send a request for further funding so that we could continue our research into cold fusion. But there was no reply on that occasion either.

"Then there was an unexpected turn of events: the High Commissioner of CEA, the government body responsible for all civilian and military nuclear activities in France contacted us. CEA had received a request from the French giant

EDF (Electricité de France) to start working on cold fusion again, and we were invited to Paris to hold seminars on this topic. Our research was greeted with considerable interest, so much so that three French scientists were sent to this very laboratory where we are now, to take photographs and make drawings of our equipment with a view to opening a similar laboratory on the outskirts of Paris. In short, they were coming all the way from France to copy our experience, when in Italy the people who had funded it were doing nothing to continue the research."[4]

"Dr. Garbati," breaks in Claudio, "Do you think you could give me any idea of what practical consequences your experiments might have?"

"You should know that we carried out experiments aimed at scientific testing and so we used metals such as palladium, which is known as white gold because of its high cost, but cold fusion can take place within several heavy metals that are much cheaper, such as tungsten, for example. Using a liter of distilled water and the full lattice of a block of tungsten only a few cubic centimeters in size, that costs only a few Euros, dozens of kilowatts of power can be produced for hundreds of years. These are the units of measure of the energy produced."

"Please continue telling me about your discovery, Dr. Garbati."

"Then there was another turn of events: on October 20th 2004, the Ministry of Economic Development called our group in. While surfing the net, they had come across Report 41, the results of our investigations and research. The Ministry said it would be interested in funding research into cold fusion, offering 800,000 Euros for two years. Of course, we were ecstatic ... but then came yet another twist. ENEA was contacted by the Ministry, accepted the funding, but decided to give it to a different group that was already following another line of research in collaboration with American and Israeli partners."

"You don't seem to have many supporters. There's probably a connection between the positive results you obtained, the disappearance of all your followers and this last loss of funds. But what interests could be affected by cold fusion?"

"Every time you do something new, you alter the balance and interests of the people who worked in the previous way. Imagine, for example, how worried the admirals of those great sailing ships must have been when the first motorized ships appeared. If you then consider that trillions of Euros had been allocated to build a huge plant (ITER) to study nuclear fusion, you can see how much cold fusion might have bothered people ..."

Claudio doesn't feel totally convinced by this explanation. In fact, after reflecting in silence for some moments, he asks, "If these were the only reasons, then your colleagues who work with the Americans and Israelis should have the same difficulties. Maybe there are other reasons ...."

The researcher becomes more serious and replies, "I suspect research has been carried out in this field for a long time by various people, some academic scholars, others in the industrial world ... others neither in the academic nor industrial field, but if I were to talk about my suspicions, I'd only make the situation worse, so I think it's best if our conversation ends here. When you run into problems with this issue, keep in mind that they may come from many different angles. And I would ask you not to mention our conversation."

"Don't worry, the camera is off. I've just taken a few notes. First I want to understand this story, then I'll see how I can tell it. Can I call you and ask for help if there's something I don't understand?"

"Of course."

"Now that *should* worry you, because it'll happen often! Here's my business card. Talk to you soon, then ..."

A little later, while he is driving towards his office, Claudio permits himself the rare pleasure of reasoning. When new information is acquired – and this doesn't happen very often – his drowsy brain synapses seem to wake up and begin a mysterious dance as they analyze the new data, predicting, making assumptions, testing.

On the other hand, what else do humans do if not make assumptions? This is their only activity: from their first day in the classroom until their last little Promethean jump, from bed to graveyard, men and women do nothing but make assumptions. And when they have nothing else to assume, they get excited about crossword puzzles, television programs. And that's what happens to Claudio as he follows the dance of hypotheses in his mind.

Professor Palazzi was right. The story is fascinating. It means doing a kind of Reverse Engineering: the deeper the research goes, the more someone will take the trouble to slow it down.

We need to know why someone is trying to hide this discovery ... we can make two hypotheses: first, that the discovery of a new source of cheap energy might scare people who up to now have earned a lot of money selling energy. Second, that behind this discovery there may be a physics process with massive potential that no one knows about, because it could lead to huge economic and military advantages. This must be the reason ... but my knowledge is ridiculously inadequate. I need to understand the physics processes better. I need ... of course, the theoretical physicist that Palazzi advised me to contact. That's who I need! I must call him, he'll undoubtedly be able to help me.

With one hand on the wheel, he pulls out his diary and keeping an eye on the road, looks for the name. "Kurt Grass. The prefix is for Tuscany. I should call him at once," he says out loud.

Chapter Three

THE PROFESSOR DREAMS ABOUT EDWARD TELLER

In some sort of crude sense, which no vulgarity, no humor, no overstatement can quite extinguish, the physicists have known sin; and this is a knowledge which they cannot lose.

– J. Robert Oppenheimer

Seen in the morning, certain hotels, like certain people, lose the subtle fascination that they exuded in the evening. The only desire they now arouse is to leave them behind as soon as possible. The professor's journey to the airport was a kind of reverse projection of the images from the previous evening, with one subtle difference: he now knew he was being followed. For this very reason, he did not want to think about it.

What difference could it possibly make if I recognize the person with the oh so boring task of following me? The real problem is another ...

The door of San Francisco airport sucked him in, anesthetizing him throughout the whole process of boarding: his only thought was to keep his place in the different lines of passengers moving towards the plane for London. But when the plane left the ground and he saw the rounded shapes of clouds beginning to float towards him through the window, then he could no longer stop his eyes from closing, as he stumbled into the shadows flurrying through his mind.

The problem is not the military, they do their work: the problem is Edward Teller. He has always been a problem for the entire scientific community. No objection to his brilliant activities as a theoretical physicist, it is his personal relationships that are a disaster. No sooner had he joined the Manhattan Project to build the nuclear bomb than he began arguing with Oppenheimer, who tried to get him involved by entrusting him with the task of creating the hydrogen bomb, in vain ... Teller waited for the right moment and then accused him of being a security risk to his country.[5] Robert Oppenheimer, the most important man at that time, responsible for building the first nuclear bomb in America. The father of the hydrogen bomb wiped out the father of the atomic bomb. After that move, the scientists who had previously wanted to work with Teller virtually disappeared. And he replaced them with the military, who became his most fervent supporters. What was it that Enrico Fermi said about Edward Teller? Ah yes, "the only monomaniac who suffers, at the same time, from multiple monomania."[6] Whereas the physicist, Isidor I. Rabi, stated that "The world would have been be a better place without Teller."[7]

When Teller accused Oppenheimer of being a member of the American Communist Party, Oppenheimer limpidly defended himself: "I have known only one member of the Communist Party: my wife, of whose dissociation from the party, integrity and loyalty to the United States I have no doubt. I have never been a member of the Communist Party. I have never accepted Communist dogma or theory, in fact, I have always considered it pointless for me."

But faced with this reply, Teller insisted, and his public declaration has gone down in history: "In a great number of cases I have seen Dr. Oppenheimer act ..... in a way which for me was exceedingly hard to understand. I thoroughly disagreed with him in numerous issues and his actions frankly appeared to me confused and complicated. To this extent I feel that I would like to see the vital interests of this country in hands which I understand better, and therefore trust more. In this very limited sense I would like to express a feeling that I would feel personally more secure if public matters would rest in other hands."[8]

At Los Alamos, the joke went round that Edward Teller's calculations for the hydrogen bomb were so wrong, that if someone passed them to the Russians they would go completely off track. Enrico Fermi, tired of receiving complaints from the other scientists about Edward Teller's tantrums, once persuaded him to write an article on the birth of the hydrogen bomb, advising him to state that it was a group project that also involved the scientist Stanislaw Ulam, which he did in fact do.[9] But soon after, he gave a second interview in which he denied the first: the H-bomb was entirely the fruit of his own work.[10]

Edward Teller never changed his way of behaving: he created a project to construct a new harbor in Alaska by exploding six nuclear devices[11], without the least concern for the local tribes. If the Canadian government had not opposed the plan, he would undoubtedly have achieved his goal. He also worked on a project that would have opened up a canal similar to the one in Panama, by using twenty-six nuclear bombs, a project which had later, thank God, been abandoned. He then became interested in how the nuclear bomb could be used for controlling the weather. But he was also a fervent supporter of the Strategic Defense Initiative, a global missile shield proposed by Ronald Reagan ... And I'm supposed to deal with a person like that? And now I have someone following me on his behalf. If the father of the hydrogen bomb decides to destroy the father of cold fusion, what chance does the latter have of surviving?

The plane continued its flight towards London while the stubborn part of the professor's brain, the part that purported to analyze and solve all problems, suggested that he hold fast, let the part of his intestine infested with tiny tumors be cut out, and quietly leave the United States.

Chapter Four

The Physicist, Kurt Grass, Talks About Alfred Coehn, A Forgotten Genius

Summer 2006. Punta Ala.

Claudio arrives on the beach where Professor Kurt Grass has arranged to meet him.

"Are you professor Kurt?"

"What makes you think I am me?"

"That's a strange way to answer, but actually it's true – I'd never have thought it was you. I imagined a seventy-year old man with glasses and a white beard."

"And not an elderly man in shorts and canvas shoes?"

"In fact, if I interviewed you with a video camera today, you wouldn't look very authoritative and the background of a seaside resort wouldn't really be suitable ..."

"I prefer not to have authority and even less suitableness, it limits the things I can say and, above all, what I can think."

"Look, I know nothing about physics and I just want some explanations, some certainty."

"Even certainties are hypotheses. You make hypotheses and around them you construct temporary and often erroneous empirical evidence that newcomers call certainties. Galileo's famous demonstration that the Earth revolved around the sun was correct as a hypothesis but wrong as a demonstration.

Enrico Fermi's discovery of two new elements, hesperium and ausonium, was completely wrong: they were two particles produced by uranium fission. So this is the typical paradox of research in the field of physics: for a mistaken discovery, Fermi received the Nobel Prize in 1938, but by using a different hypothesis based on this error, he managed to discover nuclear fission in 1939. Did he never ask himself if there was a relationship between the two things? Probably. It's all a bit more complex than what you journalists would like to think."

"Professor, could you please try to explain cold fusion to me."

"Seeing that we have also made successful hypotheses about cold fusion, but can't be absolutely certain, I'll talk as though we were walking along the way of the cross. So, at the first station of the cross we reflect upon Alfred Coehn's discovery about how hydrogen can be dissolved in metals, not in the form of neutral molecules but as ions; in the second, we contemplate the fusion of two hydrogen nuclei into a single nucleus and the discovery of cold fusion."[12]

"Go on. I'm following you."

"As I was saying, Alfred Coehn realized that hydrogen dissolves in metals, like in a sponge, but not in the form of neutral atoms or molecules – in the form of ions, i.e. nuclei devoid of electrons.[13] It had been known for a long time that hydrogen dissolved in metals, but Alfred Coehn thought about measuring the electrical resistance of that metal as hydrogen presence varied, and discovered that the number of electrons involved in the current increased with the hydrogen charge. In other words, the dissolved hydrogen supplied the metal with electrons, something that could only happen if separation occurred between the nuclei and electrons inside the molecule.

"To clarify the issue, let's look at the problem from another angle: if hydrogen didn't dissociate, the molecules dissolved in the metal would only be an obstacle to the propagation of current. Resistance should increase with an increase in the concentration of hydrogen. It turns out instead that, beyond a certain threshold, resistance begins to decrease, which is really weird."

"But why does that happen?"

"Following the line of reasoning stemming from Alfred Coehn's discovery, you arrive at the following conclusion: the increase in free electrons, as hydrogen presence increases in the metal, indicates that the hydrogen atoms split into nuclei and electrons, the electrons are released from the nuclei and go to join the other electrons flowing in the current; whereas the nuclei remain within the metal. This is the so-called *Coehn effect*.

"It was then that the Nobel laureate, Walther Hermann Nernst, wrote his famous letter in which he asserted that this was the best experiment of the century. The revolution that this discovery would entail was not lost on Nernst and it is therefore surprising that it remained buried for so long in the annals of the journal *Zeitschrift fur Elektrochemie*, precisely in volume number 35 of the year 1929 at page 676."

It is a cool summer afternoon and the light breeze off the sea makes this impromptu conference on physics most pleasant.

"And now for the second mystery: how two hydrogen nuclei fuse into one nucleus and how the discovery of cold fusion emerged. Research on the strange effects of materials charged with hydrogen, like the Coehn effect, had long been known and for some reason had an important role in the activity of military laboratories. In the '80s, Professor Fleischmann, together with his student Stanley Pons, carried out a research project on what would later be called cold fusion. His hypothesis was as follows: in the sphere of heavy metals charged with hydrogen and in particular with a hydrogen isotope, deuterium,[14] it was thought that there might be a charge level beyond which spontaneous nuclear fusions of deuterium nuclei could be generated.

"Inside the metal, electron blobs can form that are able to move unitarily with relatively autonomous movements compared to the nuclei. What would happen if these blobs allowed the positive charges of the hydrogen or deuterium nuclei to come closer to one another than in a vacuum? We must bear in mind that in a vacuum, charges of the same sign repel each other, but if the nuclei are attracted to the same blob, the so-called "pimp effect" occurs, which works like this: in the presence of a blob with a negative charge, a nucleus with a positive charge approaches from one side, another nucleus with a positive charge approaches from the other side, and both are attracted to the same blob.

"In practice, it's like watching two people standing close to each other and on the verge of a fight, but the presence of a mediator in the middle, who speaks to both parties, pulling them towards him, causes the two to come so close that eventually they can no longer see each other. In this way, a huge increase occurs in the density of the deuterium nuclei. At this point, the very magic suggested by quantum physics takes place – that had led to the formation of electron blobs, but in our case had happened with deuterium nuclei – the like likes like principle.

"When the density of a set of electrical charges exceeds a critical value, electrodynamic interactions prevail over electrostatic forces, so that the repulsive electrostatic regime is replaced by an attractive regime. Once past a critical density threshold, the deuterium nuclei – thanks to the mediation of electron blobs – instead of repelling each other, are attracted to one another. The nuclei fuse and this produces extremely high energy. So you can understand why in materials like heavy metals, which have blobs with negative charges inside them, the probability of fusion between two hydrogen or deuterium nuclei is greater than in a vacuum."

Kurt Grass stops to take a deep breath. Claudio turns around and notices that the bathers from the resort have silently gathered around Kurt Grass, listening to his seaside lesson.

Claudio realizes that Professor Grass has a very powerful voice and as soon as he starts talking about physics, his tone spontaneously settles at a volume that can easily be heard in every corner of a large lecture room. The effect is so remarkable that even the man selling coconut stops and listens, entranced, as though he were a first year student. Grass's eloquent style is rich in provocative images and full of digressions and associations, giving all those present the illusion that they have fully grasped the concept of two hydrogen atoms fusing at a low temperature. Naturally, none of them, including Claudio, would be able to repeat what they believe they have understood.

"Can I offer you an iced coffee, Professor Grass? I must say, you've made me wish I could study nuclear physics," says Claudio, breaking the spell.

"I certainly won't say no to a coffee. When do you think you'll take the exam, then, my boy?"

"It would certainly be useful and I can tell you that many people in my profession write about science, but very few really understand anything about it."

"That's the problem with the industrial society, people are just concerned with producing and not doing research, and what little we know is written and written again full of mistakes."

"But the explanation you've given me today is not sufficient. I'd like to understand better how this process might be used in the type of research which is, let's say, not academic and not even industrial."

"I suppose you're referring to military research. I think it would be better if you looked into what purposes this discovery might have for civil society. But don't worry, you can come and see me whenever you want, I never turn anyone away. And besides, you have my phone number."

"Do you think it would be possible to meet Professor Fleischmann?"

"He's a very private person, but I talk to him every now and again. If you want, I can ask if he'll let you visit him. Perhaps you don't know, but Martin lives in a cottage in England, in an area that's not easy to get to."

"I'd be happy to meet him. From his stories, he seems to be a great example of an impassioned and honest scientist."

"You'll see, before you know it, you'll be back looking for me. Have a good trip."

Chapter Five

THE NEWSROOM

After meetings of this kind, going back to the newsroom is always difficult. Claudio would like to share his enthusiasm about the story he is currently following with all his colleagues at the news channel. But as soon as he runs into a friend and begins to explain what he is working on, at the mere mention of fusion between two deuterium atoms and blobs within a lattice of metal, that person looks at his watch and says hurriedly, "I have to do an in-depth report on the Yagur protests in a quarter of an hour and I still haven't found any pictures. Sorry but I really must run."

"They're called Yugurs, actually ... Ok, off you go, we'll talk about it some other time."

So he tries to see the editor, but the office door is closed. He is in a meeting. Claudio decides to wait in the corridor and stands there watching the differing speeds at which his colleagues pass. Each sector has a different pace: the calmest and those with the most information are the Internet bunch, whereas the most agitated are the crowd from the newsroom where they are always on the air, with several teams alternating according to their shifts: the lights are eternally on. The people working there are constantly in a rush and constantly arguing about a title, an adjective or a comma. The editor suddenly comes out of his office: his phone is ringing, his secretary is calling, his driver is waiting, and he utters the sentence that he repeats whenever you meet him, "As soon as I have a moment free, I'll call you and we'll discuss it."

"Chief, I have a new story that is very ..." Claudio tries to break in.

But the editor has already started talking on his mobile phone and walks away, making a peace sign with his free hand that he will call later. A gesture that he always makes.

In the end, Claudio takes the elevator and goes down to the basement, almost happy with his underground office where he can peacefully dedicate himself to the research required by this investigation. Here he can stick photographs and cards on the bulletin board without scaring anyone, since he only has to deal with those four colleagues who, in their professional life as journalists, have learned, like him, to use a video camera and put together films on their own and, above all, travel by themselves all over the world.

They are all the result of an objective selection and have specific skills that, if you were to detail them in job announcements, might sound as follows:

"Wanted: journalists humble enough to prefer knowledge to being known.

Curious enough that they prefer traveling in foreign countries to making a career in the newsroom, stubborn enough to follow a story like bloodhounds rather than selling the first version.

Proud enough to travel at the same cost as a Franciscan monk on a visit to a monastery.

Educated enough to prefer listening to chattering.

Polite enough to be comfortable in any kind of environment.

Casual enough to be able to go to hell and talk to the devil as though he were a neighbor.

Sufficiently experienced in suffering to know how to lose rather than presuming to find something.

Determined enough to study numerous books in order to understand a single process.

Sufficiently innocent to be free of prejudice and sufficiently experienced to understand that laws do not explain much.

As ambitious as is necessary to choose a knowledge project that lasts longer than the two and a half minutes of a normal television news report."

Needless to say, from a selection of this type, only a few emerge. Claudio knows four, and has baptized them with their battle names:

Sci, from Department of Scientific Investigation, a nit-picking perfectionist who often explores two contradictory and apparently irreconcilable hypotheses in parallel and for months on end. When analyzing a document, he begins by testing the fiber of the paper used, which can be a real problem in terms of the time needed for the investigation, but makes the final results a pleasure.

Diesel, slow to get going, but once started, unstoppable. He is fiercely idiosyncratic about the office environment. When not traveling, he reads; when not reading or traveling, he jogs; and in the little time he has left, he talks, but no more than strictly necessary. Absolutely precise in timing and results.

Amba, from Ambassador, the most presentable of the group. Clearly a diplomat, he is able to change appearance according to the interviewee, and entertain the interviewee's grandparents, grandchildren and other relatives down to the third generation. His familiarity with different languages has given rise to the suspicion that he may not be Italian by birth. His charm and pleasing appearance make him particularly effective in his work, but expose him to the risk of being kidnapped by directors fans of video presenters, who he avoids like the plague.

Cass, from Cassandra, an endangered species, both because of her age and her specific behavior as a conspiracy prophet: due to her experience and refined intuition, she guarantees foreknowledge of any news item by several years, so much so that her contributions are virtually unusable in the newsroom. She spends most of her time reading, talking to herself or holding conferences with tiny audiences, and sometimes she get hugely excited by news that is irrelevant or totally insignificant for the rest of humanity. She blurts out predictions that are regularly and carefully recorded by her biographers, and then put aside until enough years have passed for them to be finally taken into consideration.

These are Claudio's true confidants and it could not be otherwise. They are the only people who know all the details of each other's work, ready to substitute one another or work side by side in every stage of production, where they exchange voices, cameras, ideas, video editors and music.

Chapter Six

THE PROFESSOR GOES UNDER THE KNIFE

Who cannot be crushed with a plot? ...
Yet am I thankful: if my heart were great,
'Twould burst at this. Captain I'll be no more;
But I will eat and drink, and sleep as soft
As captain shall: simply the thing I am
Shall make me live. Who knows himself a braggart,
Let him fear this, for it will come to pass
that every braggart shall be found an ass.
Rust, sword? cool, blushes! and, Parolles, live
Safest in shame! being fool'd, by foolery thrive!
There's place and means for every man alive.
I'll after them.

—Shakespeare, *All's Well That Ends Well*,
London 1989.

Who said that one shot of an anesthetic is enough to forget? Anesthesia has the opposite effect: it makes you remember without feeling pain, experience life as though in a dream, with every detail perfectly clear.

"Please give me your left arm, Professor. When this liquid starts to circulate, you'll already be asleep."

I don't think I'm quite asleep, at least not yet ...

I'm just remembering. My first getaway ... I was eleven when my father was brutally beaten by the Gestapo ... Then the taxi, my father was sitting in front, next to the driver who was a fellow fighter, a friend of his who had decided to drive us out of Czechoslovakia, not yet completely occupied by the Na-

zis, in one of his company cars. That day, the sky was a special color, I seem to see it even now, it's like I'm still there.

When you are on the run and driving a car, you hold the steering wheel in a different way, you watch the road in another way, and even though I was still small, I realized it. And at the same time, I sensed something else, much more important – friendship, the strength of that genuine feeling ... this friend was risking his life to help us. There was something powerful in that action, something I have not forgotten in all these years.

And when Czechoslovakia finally fell, the second escape, this time by train. The railroad cars stationary on the border with Holland, and my father quietly ordering, "Don't move from your seat!" while the Nazis search the whole train, compartment by compartment, looking for people seeking safety in flight. It's as though I can still hear the sound of doors opening, the harsh orders shouted in German. Then the miracle: they were a mere step away from our compartment, the very last ... the Nazis were searching the one just before ours when the train began to move and they had to jump down.

And then, finally arriving at Liverpool Street Station: with just 27 shillings and 26 pence in our pockets, for four people. The end of my life, my first death. I cannot relate the painfulness of that moment – my sister adopted by a Methodist minister, and I myself staying with the minister's unmarried brother-in-law.

... I really don't think I've fallen asleep, I can hear the surgeons' voices as they open my stomach and fiddle around with my intestine ... which is what I'm doing with my memory ... I'd rather sleep, but I'm oppressed by memories and I have to dream, I cannot resist ...

Suddenly, an explosion in the night, and then a fire ... one of my first experiments: I'm charging a cell, but perhaps I shouldn't have done it. And yet, all the subsequent developments in my research came from that precise discovery, from that explosion which destroyed the laboratory table with the cell on it, and made a hole in the floor right down to the floor below; all my research studies started from the exceptional heat caused by that cubic centimeter of metal, trying to understand the process by which it was given off. Five long years of isolated work ... and then suddenly catapulted onto television screens throughout the world ... and then insulted and derided ... and now, if my operation goes well, time to run away again, keep a low profile, be isolated ...

But I had to, I just had to do it before this operation, I had to let people know that there was a system for creating energy independence, a system with laughably low costs that can work anywhere, in any climate and on every continent ... and now if they insult and discredit me, I will anyway survive.

How many times can a man die? How many times can he survive? How many times can I still find poison in my intestine?

How many pieces of intestine will I still have? And what will happen to my friends who are following me in this adventure, who understand what is at stake and yet don't give up on this dangerous game? They might also have radioactive dust, with no smell or taste, put in their glasses, in their food ... How much longer can scientists pretend they don't know, for how much longer will people avoid talking in lecture halls and laboratories about this energy, tell lies to conceal the physics processes that are behind these discoveries?

"Professor, can you hear me? The surgery went well, you must rest now, only rest and you'll see, everything will be just like it was before."

Just like it was before would be difficult. Because the intestine doesn't grow on its own, because if it's true that I was poisoned, I can no longer pretend that I don't know. And if it's true that I was followed, I can't pretend I don't know that, or expect to be always among friends. And if I was accused of falsifying the result of the experiments, I can't hope to be nominated again for the Nobel prize for chemistry.

I can at least be happy that I'm still alive, and I am, but don't tell me that everything will be just like it was before, because that's not true.

Chapter Seven

PRESS CONFERENCE IN SALT LAKE CITY ON MARCH 23, 1989

In the newsroom, Claudio is staring at the photos of Fleischmann and Pons on the bulletin board.

"Can I steal a few moments of your precious time?" he asks at a certain point.

"Only if you take it off our work schedule," says Diesel.

"I'm serious. This issue is extremely interesting, but very complicated. It has scientific and historical aspects about which we know absolutely nothing. All the success and prizes we've won in recent years have been achieved through team work. None of us could have done it alone. Let's deal with this investigation together, too, we can divide the work like we always do. I've already prepared a table on cold fusion. It's in your email: this is rather a prickly subject and it'd be better if all of us tried to understand something about it, so that we can work together. Let me just read it to you quickly: "From 1984 to 1989, the English professor Martin Fleischmann and his American colleague Stanley Pons worked in great secrecy on the possibility of producing a nuclear reaction at a low temperature[15] creating a thermally well-insulated container and filling it with so-called "heavy water."[16] In this container, they then immersed two electrodes, one made of palladium and the other of platinum. By passing current through them, they managed to produce heat, in the vicinity of the palladium, that in energy terms is greater than the energy supplied by the battery.

Overall, they produced a power of 4 watts compared to the one watt supplied by the battery, so with a yield of 400%. Furthermore, in the course of this activity, they derived helium, small traces of tritium, neutrons and other forms of energy such as gamma rays and X rays."

"Sorry, Claudio," breaks in Sci. "Which universities were they working at?"

"You're quite right, I didn't put that down – the University of Utah. Stanley Pons, who had been Fleischmann's pupil, taught there, and Fleischmann had come to see him with the idea of collaborating. So ... "The two scientists, after they had spent all their free time and about 100 thousand dollars of their savings in those five years, decided to ask the U.S. Department of Energy for funding to continue their research. And that's when the problems began. Among the government officials from that department who would be in charge of funding the grant, there was also Professor Steve E. Jones from Brigham Young University in Provo, Utah, who had tried to achieve cold fusion using a different process.[17] Jones had already published an article entitled 'Cold fusion' in the July 1987 issue of the Scientific American magazine."

"Sorry to interrupt you, but the term 'cold fusion', even if discredited today, was actually coined for the first time by Steve E. Jones?" asks Amba.

"I think so, even if the method described by Jones was very different from that of Fleischmann and Pons and no one has ever filed a patent for the term 'cold fusion'. Anyway, they managed to reach some sort of agreement: "The three professors met and studied the results of the experiments in detail: Fleischmann and Pons were pushed by the University of Utah to patent the possible commercial exploitation of this discovery, whereas Jones seemed to be more interested in the figures concerning the production of neutrons and much less concerned about the patent. On March 6, 1989 they all agreed to publish two articles in the same issue of the journal Nature, making an appointment for March 24 at the Federal Express office in Salt Lake City airport to send the material at the same time."

"Does it seem professionally correct to you that someone who is controlling funding should become involved in the publication of research whose validity he's supposed to be verifying?" queries Cass aggressively.

"The real problems have yet to emerge. Up to this point, the versions of the three professors coincide, but now they begin to diverge: "According to Jones, it went without saying that up to March 24, none of the three would utter a word about what they had discovered; according to Fleischmann and Pons, however, there had been no agreement regarding non-disclosure and, under pressure from the Rector at the University of Utah, who did not want to miss out on the patent for a discovery that seemed very promising from the commercial point of view, they were forced to do two things which Professor Jones deemed improper: first, on 11 March 1989, they sent a brief announcement about cold fusion to the Journal of Electroanalytical Chemistry; second, they convened an impromptu press conference on March 23, during which, in front of journalists from all over the world, they announced the possibility of fusing two deuterium nuclei at room temperature."

"I just want to repeat that a person controlling funding cannot be involved in the project that he is analyzing," insists Cass.

"Fleischmann and Pons, as agreed, went to the Federal Express office on 24 March to send the articles, but obviously did not find Jones who, furious about their press conference, had already arranged to send his paper by fax to the editorial board at Nature."

"Despite the turmoil unleashed by them anticipating the news, I think the real problem was the fact that the data was not yet complete," breaks in Amba. "Or am I wrong?"

"In fact, the press conference was called in a hurry and, what's more, on a subject that was extremely delicate from various points of view – academic, commercial, strategic, it was immediately at the center of a battle with no holds barred.

"This decision to accelerate had two main outcomes. The first was to make known the work of Fleischmann and Pons and thus prevent someone else from taking the credit for having invented cold fusion before them. Don't imagine that there were no interested stakeholders: for example, the University of Boston: Massachusetts Institute of Technology announced nearly a month later, that it had applied for a patent on the same argument based on the theoretical work of the researcher, Peter L. Hagelstein,[18] who had hurried to submit articles for the next issues of the journal, on April 5 and 12. But this decision to speed things up had the effect of creating an air of total delegitimization around cold fusion."

"But other than these quarrels, had the methods of the experiment been quite clearly stated?" asks Sci.

"Thanks also to its preliminary nature, Fleischmann and Pons' work laid itself open to a number of criticisms which, in most cases, stemmed from misunderstandings. In any case, the central phenomenon of cold fusion had been identified with sufficient clarity, as had the new approach to the underlying nuclear process.[19]

"The two scientists had only been able to give reliable measurements about the energy consumed and produced, but they did not have suitable instruments to register the particles produced in the nuclear process. For this reason, they had asked the local university's Department of Physics to lend them some instruments so that they could identify the reaction products that usually appear in the processes of hot fusion.[20] The reproducibility of the experiment was however clearly linked to reaching critical threshold concentration."

"Did the other laboratories that unsuccessfully attempted the experiment provide their data on hydrogen charging?" interrupts Diesel.

"You must understand that none of the experimental groups, which in 1989-90 reported their failure to reproduce the experiment, ever disclosed the charge level that was reached, so the possibility remains that this failure was due to the fact that the threshold was not reached. When, after a long series of experiments, the ENEA group provided this data,[21] the problem was solved and the reproducibility condition clarified."

"But I heard there was a real campaign to delegitimize Fleischmann and Pons ..." said Amba.

"True. Particularly in the United States, where the Department of Energy and its associated universities and journals greatly contributed to delegitimizing the discovery of cold fusion. But there were also clear cases of data being manipulated, like the case that Eugene Mallove reported.[22] I'll tell you later what happened."

"Oh no, you can tell us right now!" insists Amba.

"No, it's complicated and we should look at it together with the other elements, we'll talk about it later. Now let's take a step back in time and have a look at what happened immediately after the announcement about cold fusion.

"On April 12 1989, Stanley Pons gave a very successful presentation at the annual Congress of the American Chemical Society and soon after the University of Utah asked the US Congress for $25 million funding to carry out new research. In Washington, our two scientists also met senior administration officials.

"But along with fame came controversy, too. A few weeks later, it was the turn of the annual Congress for the American Physical Society, and here things went differently. Perhaps because the physicists at the conference were moved by a sort of corporate spirit and annoyed by this sensational discovery which was the work of two chemists, they triggered a crossfire of criticism. The national laboratories of Brookhaven and Yale University presented the data on the failed reproducibility of the cold fusion experiment: not only was excess energy not produced, but not even neutrons. This chorus of criticism was then swelled by that of researchers from laboratories in Harwell, near Oxford, in the UK. In November, it was the turn of a special group of scientists from the US Department of Energy (DOE) who, after studying the phenomenon, issued a negative ruling. Towards the end of the year, the term used to define cold fusion was a 'phenomenon of pseudoscience'.

"In the nineties, paradoxically, it was the European and Asian scientists who supported research into cold fusion by coming up with positive results. The first criticisms also began to emerge about the rapid and biased ditching of this extraordinary discovery. Among the most respected authorities, there was also the Nobel laureate Julian Schwinger, who admitted that many editors of scientific journals had been subjected to heavy pressure aimed at casting cold fusion in a bad light."

"We could try to interview him," Diesel tosses in.

"Too late. He died in 1994. Now I'll finish the story.

"Paradoxically, the military were the first to favorably reconsider cold fusion. In February 2002, a report by the U.S. Navy took stock of the cold fusion created by the U.S. Navy between 1989 and 2002, revealing that an excess of heat and helium 4 had been produced in the experiments, as a result of the nuclear processes occurring inside the cell.[23] In December 2004, the Department of Energy itself sponsored an analysis on cold fusion.[24] The Ministry of Energy commissioned a group of scientists to review the scientific evidence for low energy nuclear reactions.[25] All the material was then evaluated according to a complex protocol. This is a summary of the conclusions: "In the final analysis, the reviewers did not come to a conclusion on the existence of cold fusion and therefore recommend that new research methods be identified, which may address the uncertainties in the previously found/original results."

"In short, the U.S. Navy seemed more open than the Department of Energy. I wonder why?" says Cass sarcastically.

"Yeah, I wonder."

Chapter Eight

TUTANKHAMEN'S CURSE

After several phone calls with no answer, Claudio finally contacts Professor Kurt Grass again. This time, he has to get the interview on film. They make an appointment to meet in his office at the university.

"I didn't know that theoretical physicists had such tiny offices. It's almost impossible to squeeze in a camera, its stand and the interviewee at the same time," jokes Claudio.

"When you have an office, you're not happy. When you have the sea in the background, you're not happy either. In short, you never know what you want ..." retorts the professor.

Claudio notes with pleasure that the professor is now using the familiar "you" form, but decides that he will continue to use the polite form, so as not to make mistakes during the interview.

"I just need a whiteboard in the background."

"Well, it's mainly theoretical physicists who use them. Let's go and look for one."

As the noise of their footsteps echoes down the corridors of the University, Claudio takes up the discussion that had been interrupted several weeks before.

"Why is there always this 'conspiracy theory' atmosphere when it comes to cold fusion? It always seems that there's someone hiding in the shadows ready to stand in your way, spy on you or threaten you ..."

"I call it the curse of Tutankhamen."

"What do you mean?"

"Tutankhamen ruled Egypt for ten years or so, from 1333 to 1323 BC. He was not a particularly enlightened or active ruler, he only reigned for a short time and he was too young when he died to go down in history. You may remember him, because he is portrayed together with his wife in the statues at Luxor. Those statues are interesting, too, because after Tutankhamen's death, his successor, Ramses II, replaced the stone scrolls belonging to that couple with his own and those of his wife, Nefertari. In other words, to save money, he changed the names on the inscriptions of their statues instead of building two new ones. As you can see, copyright issues already existed a thousand years before Christ. I know you think that what I'm telling you has nothing to do with cold fusion, but if you're patient, you'll see what the connection is.

"Tutankhamen died at the age of 19-20, probably after falling off a chariot, which led to a tetanus infection and his subsequent death from septicemia. His tomb, one of many in the Valley of the Kings, was discovered in 1922 by Howard Carter. And the archaeologist, who had been exploring that area for ten years, was lucky because it was almost intact and crammed with all kinds of riches, thrones, weapons, jewelry. Carter was relieved, because his research had been financed throughout that time by an English lord, the Earl of Carnarvon, who until then had been losing money.

"In reality, what made Tutankhamen's tomb famous was not so much its treasure, as its curse. A few months after the discovery, as the Earl of Carnarvon was shaving, he re-opened a small sore caused by an insect bite. After a very short time, an infection spread throughout his body, until he was so debilitated that he was finally killed by a simple case of pneumonia. This death was enough to start the legend of Tutankhamen's curse. In reality, of the 26 people present when the tomb was opened, only six died in the following ten years, and Carter himself did not die until he was sixty-five, some seventeen years later. Was it really a curse? We'll never know, but you can be sure that when Tutankhamen's name is mentioned, it is above all in reference to this curse. And this is the point: the truth is that everything started with Lord Carnarvon's decision to grant exclusive rights about the discovery of Tutankhamen's tomb to only one American newspaper. The other newspapers were very resentful about this and began to sow doubts as to whether this discovery was really true. So in the end, when Carnarvon died so unexpectedly, everyone began to speak about the curse of the tomb as though it were a sort of revenge. But the truth is that it was not so much Tutankhamen's revenge as that of the newspapers which had been left without information.

"I think there is some sort of analogy to what happened with cold fusion. The fact that it was announced so quickly, without considering the reaction it would provoke in all those people engaged in research on hot fusion, or the fear of the military who were studying similar processes with other materials, or even the greed of dozens of researchers and academic institutions that were carrying out research on this subject, all of this created such a wide-ranging and unified coalition to delegitimize that in the end, despite the fact that cold fusion really exists, it will be remembered as a kind of cursed topic that cannot even be mentioned."

"In this case, however, nobody died from the curse, did they?"

"That's not quite true. There were strange episodes that may likewise fuel this conspiracy theory. First episode: Professor Martin Fleischmann, who had already informed the Department of Energy about his work on room temperature nuclear reactions, discovered that a part of his intestine had been attacked by hundreds of little tumors, which may have been compatible with poisoning by very localized radioactive dust. I don't know what he thought when he heard about the disease, but no sooner had he decided to publicize his discovery than he started getting strange phone calls, which could be seen as threats. So, he had the operation in England and the surgery on his intestine was successful.

"Something similar also happened to an Italian scientist, the theoretical physicist who formulated the hypothesis that was most likely to explain cold fusion. To his great surprise, he was invited to dinner by an eminent scientist, who was known to be close to some military bodies in a country where those groups are particularly powerful. During this dinner, so it was said, the host had spoken at length to his Italian colleague, complimenting him on his studies. About a year later, hundreds of small tumors were found in the Italian professor's intestine, too. Discovered too late, they were the cause of his death in 2000.

"Then there was the strange death of Eugene Mallove, an outstanding researcher who graduated from MIT in Boston[26] but resigned in protest, after discovering that the data on cold fusion had been deliberately altered in a publication.[27]

"He was beaten to death on May 14, 2004 in Norwich, Connecticut, while he was doing repair work on his parents' house. The local police classed his death as due to a robbery that had gone wrong, even though nothing was stolen. The charges against the two suspects were dropped in 2008. In February 2009, the state of Connecticut promised a reward of $50,000 for anyone giving information that would lead to the arrest or indictment of Eugene Mallove's murderer.

"Plunging even deeper into paranoia, we can also recall that the high commissioner of the French CEA, Professor René Pellat, fifteen days after speaking with the group of Italian scientists who had worked at the Frascati ENEA, suddenly died of a heart attack while swimming in the sea.[28] The only thing that goes against this conspiracy hypothesis is this: when I was twenty, I had my fortune told by a gypsy, who predicted that I would have an exceptionally long life."

"I think if someone wanted to, they could easily develop a conspiracy theory with everything that you've told me. But I'm interested in facts not suppositions."

"I know you despise suppositions stick only to the facts. But today you're here asking me who might be interested in withholding information from the public about cold fusion research."

"That's true, and I'd really like to know your opinion."

"So I'll answer in riddles. You think about it and then we'll talk. What do you think would happen if instead of charging deuterium in a metal like palladium, you chose uranium, the heaviest metal in the table of elements? Well, now we can get on with the interview, during which I will obviously not talk about these things."

Chapter Nine

THE PROFESSOR'S CONVALESCENCE

Since the professor had come out of the operating room, the word "life" had taken on new meaning for him. First of all, it went way beyond his person: life was no longer only his, but stretched to all the organisms that surrounded him, plants certainly, animals, but also the sky, seemingly so immense and yet so slight. Then, the English countryside in autumn helped him to frame existence from another point of view: that of the seasons, of the cold which became more intense every day, of the objects forgotten in drawers, like a certificate of merit ...

So I was awarded a prize by the Electrochemical Society of the United States: a medal made from palladium... why palladium, I wonder ... truly an ironic prize ... if it hadn't been given to me in 1985, perhaps my story would be different ... and it was in fact the palladium from that medal which I used for my first experiments ...

But in the drawer, the professor also found a medal awarded by the Royal Society of Chemists for his studies on electrochemistry and thermodynamics ...

Being a member of the Royal Society doesn't seem to have helped me much... it hasn't protected me from danger or from being shadowed ...

Every now and again, he found himself thinking about everything that had happened to him, now that, steeped in the silence of his home, he had a little time to put together the facts and analyze them. But there was still something he could not understand: a comment by Edward Teller on the day after the announcement about cold fusion which read: "It seems extremely promising ... my initial opinion was that it could never happen. I am very happy because I see a good chance that I was completely wrong."[29]

How should I view this? In formal terms, they offer positive feedback... Except that Teller's assessments of new scientific facts, especially when positive, are always accompanied by two riders: the first that he already knows about the fact, and the second that he does not think it can work. And once he has said this, he can then pretend that he is happy about his eventual mistake. This kind of reasoning is an integral part of his psychological makeup. Yet, in these sentences I just cannot see any interest in me that would justify shadowing me or explain the concern that the military might have about my activity.

Then there was the meeting in Washington that took place October 15-18, sponsored by the National Science Foundation and the Electric Power Research Institute, and was attended by fifty scientists. On that occasion, Teller, faced with sure evidence of the production of heat, neutron and tritium, hazarded the hypothesis that the phenomenon could be caused by an unknown neutral particle, which he called "meshoganon," from the Yiddish word 'meshuga' which means crazy. He also suggested testing uranium-235 in its capacity to "support" cold fusion and trying to replace the deuterium nucleus with beryllium. In the end, he proposed that they recognize it as being a work of great class, which had produced surprising results and that they should support the effort necessary to discover if these results were due to sophisticated difficulties or to a truly unknown phenomenon.

These sentences do not, however, seem at all "innocent" to me.

To tell the truth, the attempt to keep everything quiet, invoking the birth of a new neutral particle, reminds me of another very strange episode: the famous, and very controversial, error made by Enrico Fermi who, after he had experienced fission in his Italian experiments, declared that "he had not noticed" and that he had mistaken it for the birth of two new particles, ausonium and hesperium. According to some Italian physicists who, in this case, are my friends, we could say it was a deliberate error – Fermi did not want Mussolini to get his hands on the enormous energy potential of the fission bomb. And if he had not hidden his discovery, thanks to that barely believable error, the course of history would have been different. But in the end, someone noticed: Hector Majorana seems to have raised the subject during a noisy quarrel with Fermi, trading the term "moron" with the future Nobel laureate on several occasions. It was such a glaring error that, for many years, the caretaker of that laboratory in via Panisperna, repeatedly told the students about it.

And perhaps even Majorana's death has something to do with this error, which might not have been an error. It also amazes me that the Nobel jury accepted Fermi's discovery, thus allowing him to leave Italy forever under the pretext of receiving a prize that he had been given for a false discovery ... in short, a bizarre story!

And now, the fact that Teller, the very same scientist who had me shadowed, should state that my work is interesting but is probably related to the discovery of a new neutral particle, and then suggests experimenting with uranium ... well, this all seems to confirm the fact that someone is trying to hide, a little clumsily, a discovery whose impact has clearly been underestimated.

Chapter Ten

A LESSON IN
NUCLEAR PHYSICS

The meeting had been arranged at a restaurant in Frascati.

"What time does the lesson start?" asks Sci. "Do we have to be absolutely punctual?"

"Do I have time to order a bowl of pasta and beans?" inquires Diesel.

"Will there be a break after the first hour?" queries Amba.

"Stop bothering me," replies Claudio. "We just have to ask some questions about radiation and do a crash course on how to use a Geiger counter. Shouldn't take more than four hours max."

Putting together four reporters who are usually on four opposite sides of the world, is already a hard task. And if the meeting has been called for the purpose of following a lesson on radiation with Dr. Garbati, the situation risks getting entirely out of hand. But as soon as the questions begin, things start looking interesting.

"Dr. Garbati, can you explain how one spots radiation?" begins Claudio.

"There are basically three types: alpha, beta and gamma," answers the woman. "The first is a charged nucleus with a low penetration power highly ionizing form of particle radiation (i.e. able to rip electrons from the atoms) and with low penetration power. Alpha radiation is typically emitted by the radioactive nuclei of heavy elements, for example by the isotopes of uranium, thorium, and radium. Due to their electrical charge, alpha rays interact strongly with matter and can therefore only travel for a few centimeters through the air. Alpha particles (even if they are very ionizing) cannot penetrate layers of matter thicker than a sheet of paper. They can be absorbed by the outer layers of human skin and so are not generally life threatening, unless the emission source is inhaled or swallowed. In that case the damage would be greater than any other type of ionizing radiation, and if the dosage were high enough, all the typical symptoms of radiation poisoning would appear.

"Beta radiation is a form of ionizing radiation emitted by certain types of radioactive nuclei such as cobalt-60. This type of radiation takes the form of electrons or high-energy positrons, ejected from an atomic nucleus. The interaction of beta particles with matter generally has a range of action ten times greater than that of alpha particles, with an ionizing power equivalent to one tenth. Beta particles can be completely blocked by a few millimeters of aluminum.

"Gamma rays are a form of electromagnetic radiation produced by radioactivity or other nuclear or subatomic processes. They are more penetrating than either alpha or beta radiation, but less ionizing. They differ from X-rays in their origin: gamma rays are produced by nuclear or anyway subatomic transitions, whereas X-rays are produced by energy transitions caused by the rapid movement of electrons. *Shielding* from *gamma rays* requires *very thick shields.* In order to reduce the intensity of a gamma ray by 50%, you need 1 cm of lead, 6 cm of concrete or 9 cm of packed soil. Even though gamma rays are less ionizing than alpha or beta rays, thicker screens are needed to protect human beings. Gamma rays produce effects similar to those caused by X-rays, such as burns, forms of cancer and genetic mutations. But don't forget that natural radioactivity can be found everywhere on Earth. Natural background radiation is due to radioactive isotopes of natural elements found in the earth's crust, as well as cosmic radiation. The total worldwide *average* effective *dose* absorbed by a human being from *natural radiation* is approximately 2.4 millisieverts (mSv) per year. This figure is used as a reference for estimating the risk of pollution, but the level of natural background radiation varies significantly from place to place. In Italy, for example, the average dose equivalent rate estimated for the population is 3.4 mSv per year, but there are geographical areas where natural background radiation is significantly higher than the world average, such as Ramsar in Iran, where peak yearly doses of 260 mSv have been recorded.

"In its initial stage, in the minutes or hours following irradiation, radiation poisoning is not usually fatal. This phase lasts from a period of several hours to several days during which there are symptoms like diarrhea, nausea, vomiting, anorexia, skin inflammation. Then comes a period in which the person appears to be in good shape. Finally, the acute phase arrives with a complex series of symptoms, generally characterized by disorders affecting the skin, blood, gastro-intestinal, respiratory and cerebrovascular systems."

"Excuse me, Doctor Garbati," asks Sci, interrupting the explanation. "The Commission on depleted uranium has deliberately fired missiles containing so-called depleted uranium and then come across materials on the blast site that are different from those found previous to the explosion, such as strontium and gold, produced by fissile elements, and other materials compatible with the fission origin of materials. How is that possible?"[30]

"There may be two explanations. First: that these materials were already present in so-called depleted uranium and so the missile was constructed with waste products from nuclear reactors. Second: that such materials are the result of a micro fission which took place at the moment of the explosion."

"Are these two explanations mutually exclusive?" queries Sci.

"Not at all. In fact, the increased presence of radioactive materials under particular conditions such as a very heavy increase in pressure could in fact provoke micro fission explosions and the release of high energy in various forms, including that of heat transmission."

"If your first hypothesis is correct, it shouldn't be called depleted uranium, but dirty or reprocessed uranium," says Diesel, breaking into the discussion.

"You're right, depleted uranium should never have been put into a nuclear reactor."

"Can you explain the difference between depleted uranium, enriched uranium and natural uranium?" asks Amba.

"Uranium is one of the 92 chemical elements found in nature. The atoms of each element, including uranium, always have the same number of protons, but can have a different number of neutrons. These atoms are called isotopes. In nature, every substance occurs as a " blend" of several isotopes. For uranium, 99.3% of this blend is composed of uranium 238, and the other 0.7% is uranium 235.

"Starting with natural uranium, which can be extracted from mineral deposits, it is possible to create two metal derivatives in the laboratory: enriched uranium (more radioactive and containing more uranium-235 nuclei) and depleted uranium (containing fewer uranium-235 nuclei). Both are created by putting the uranium into a gaseous form and passing it through centrifuges that separate uranium-238 from uranium-235. In this way, the percentage of uranium-235, which is the more unstable and radioactive of the two, can be increased to above 0.7%, and then enriched uranium will be obtained; but if it is below 0.7%, then depleted uranium will be obtained.

"Because of its high density, depleted uranium is used to make shields for highly radioactive sources and as counterweights for aircraft, helicopters and sailing boats. It is often claimed, even though there is no apparent proof, that depleted uranium could have military applications because of its high density, serving in the production of projectiles capable of making particular impact with a target. The military would use depleted uranium because it is a waste byproduct of enriched uranium production that cannot be used for anything else and is therefore, relatively inexpensive, whereas enriched uranium is used in nuclear reactors as well as for the production of nuclear bombs."

"So if fissile materials are found after the explosion of projectiles, the uranium used should not be of the depleted variety, right?" breaks in Claudio.

"Exactly," replies the doctor.

"Would it be correct to call it dirty?" asks Sci.

"Officially, it's dirty and probably more radioactive than the threshold of 0.7% because it contains other fissile materials."

"So why do they keep calling it depleted uranium?" asks Diesel.

"Ask the military, not me. I'm not exactly sure what type of uranium is used in military weapons. And I also thought that, elements produced by fission had emerged from the test conducted by the Parliamentary Committee, but bear the second hypothesis in mind, too, namely that micro-fission may have occurred on impact."

"From the physics standpoint, could the explosion of tons of projectiles made from spent nuclear fuel be defined as a dirty nuclear bomb?" asks Sci.

"If it's made of material that is even low-level radioactive, then in fact it is. Now let me move on and explain how to use a Geiger counter and emphasize the importance of assessing background radiation to estimate how radioactive a particular area is. You're concerned with weapons and just by increasing background radiation, it can be difficult to perceive an increase in specific radioactivity. It's equally difficult to measure the radioactivity of dust if, at the same time, dust with a percentage of uranium-235 above or below 0.7% is used. Don't forget that there's also a margin of error for the instruments, which is as much as 15% for some, and so it's difficult to be sure of the presence of uranium-235, if precautions are taken to hide the fact that it's being used."

The lesson lasts much longer than expected and the questions, answers and deductions open up fascinating scenarios. On the other hand, it would be naïve to think that war is a fair battle with no false pretenses or deceptions.

Chapter Eleven

J.B. Conant: War Administrator, President of Harvard, and the Groves Memorandum

They create machines those people there and a machine can really be used only when it has become independent of the scientific thought that led to its invention. And so nowadays any moron can make an electric light bulb explode or detonate a nuclear bomb.

–Friedrich Dürrenmatt, *The Physicists*

Entering the investigative newsroom, Claudio throws his backpack on the table just as Sci is beginning to read his research to the others.

"This is a memorandum sent on October 30, 1943 by James Bryant Conant, President of the National Defense Research Committee for the United States, and two Nobel laureates, Arthur H. Compton and Harold C. Urey, to Brigadier General L. R. Groves, at that time director of the Manhattan Project."

"You're right on track with the news. October 30, 1943 ... you've got quite a way to go until 2006," jokes Claudio.

"Don't be stupid, this document is extremely important ... I found it while I was doing research on the Internet about depleted uranium," says Sci.

"Go on," urges Claudio.

"It's a report 'on the use of radioactive materials as a military weapon,' according to which radioactive material would first be broken into microscopic particles to form dust, and then inserted into projectiles for ground weapons or aerial bombs. It'd take only a very small quantity to cause the death of a person who inhaled it. It's been estimated that one millionth of a gram accumulated in a person's body would be enough to kill them and there's no treatment of any kind. Two factors seem to increase the vicious effectiveness of radioactive dust or fumes: the fact that they can't be perceived by the senses and that they are microscopic, which enables them to pass through even the filters of gas masks in sufficiently harmful quantities.

"In addition, radioactive material is so finely pulverized that it behaves much like a gas and is therefore subject to all the factors, like the wind, which cause it to be rapidly dispersed outside the area immediately involved. The recommendations drafted by the subcommittee order detailed studies to be carried out on the topic immediately, should radioactive weapons be used by the enemy, with the aim of preparing similar arsenals to be used by the military authorities in the United States. The uses that the military foresees for these materials are as soil pollutants: should the enemy take control of the territory, they would be dispersed throughout the area by land or air. Daily exposure (100 roentgen over the entire surface of the body) would cause temporary disability, whereas exposure for a whole week would lead to death. The effects would probably not be immediate, but delayed for days or weeks, depending on the period of exposure. If exposure were five to ten times higher, the people involved would become disabled in a couple of days, whereas if it were to continue for a period of three to five days, the damage would be more consistent, with fatal

47

consequences. Contamination of the areas would persist until the radioactive material slowly and naturally decayed, which could take weeks or even months. Where hard, flat surfaces existed, initial decontamination could be achieved by using water, but for medium-type lands, no decontamination method is yet known. It seems there is no existing type of clothing that can protect the personnel employed in operational activities and no treatment methods that will effectively counteract this type of problem. These materials are also able to contaminate the body through ingestion. Water reservoirs, wells or even food itself can be 'treated,' with effects similar to those caused by inhalation of the dust or fumes.

"Four days of production could supply enough radioactive material to contaminate one million gallons of water, and a quarter of a gallon drunk every day would probably lead to disability or death within a month. Although only fragmentary information is available, it's likely that the initial symptoms occur with bronchial irritation after only a few hours or days following exposure, depending on the dose. Immediate disability would occur with doses close to 400 or more roentgen per day. Permanent damage would be seen after some months, caused by the constant, if slow, irradiation of ingested particles. It seems that skin surfaces and lungs would be most rapidly and efficiently affected by chemical gases. Beta radiation emissions would on the other hand have more permanent effects that would appear even months after exposure. The fission products that emit beta radiation could get into the gastrointestinal tract via contaminated water and foodstuffs, or through the air, spreading from the nose to the throat and then into the bronchial tubes, until they are swallowed. The effects would be like a localized irritation in the stomach, cecum and rectum, where substances remain longer than in any other organ.

"Ulcers and perforations of the intestine would probably also appear, leading to death, even without the typical effects of radioactive contamination. After having been absorbed by the lungs or the gastrointestinal tract, fission products, emitters of gamma rays, would flow into the blood, spreading throughout the entire body. The report concludes with the usual warning 'This document contains information concerning U.S. national defense according to Espionage Act, U.S.C. 50:31 and 32. Transmission or disclosure of the information contained herein to an unauthorized person in any way whatsoever is prohibited by the law.'"

"When was it declassified?" asks Claudio.

"Only in 1974."

"It seems like a very detailed request for authorization. It describes in almost prophetic terms the symptoms that then appeared in the so-called "Gulf War syndrome" in 1991, when depleted uranium projectiles were used for the first time. So at the highest levels of the military administration, the dangers of contamination by breathing or swallowing radioactive micro or nano particles, were already fully known, given that the report specifies that they emit alpha radiation, just like depleted uranium."

"It also specifies that they can be used to poison food and water ..."

"The perfect crime – no causal and temporal relationship between the poisoning and the onset of symptoms, which occurs much later and in a stochastic manner."

"And who was this perfect gentleman who theorized radioactive dust as a weapon?"

"That's the most horrific aspect: the Groves Memorandum was written by James Bryant Conant, who was President of Harvard University, educational administrator and United States government official, Chairman of the National Defense Research Committee and Ambassador to Germany."

"So much for the independence of academia. Did you prepare a file on him? If so, I'd like to see what he looks like."

"So, his contact with Harvard began when he studied in the Faculty of Chemistry. Then after his PhD, he continued teaching Organic Chemistry and Physics there. During the early stages of the First World War, Conant didn't hide his liking of the Germans, at least until the moment when 'mustard gas' appeared on the battlefields, used by Germany against the French infantry in open violation of the Hague Convention.[31] It was then that Conant offered his services to the War Office as a chemist, later becoming responsible for the supervision of a secret laboratory where Lewisite gas projectiles were produced. His university career benefited from these services rendered to the nation and in 1933 he was offered the position of President at Harvard University, which he held until 1953. During those years, he transformed the university, imposing an entrance examination for high school students based on a test that measured aptitude, which was then adopted in many other American colleges, and launching a total revamping of teaching methods, gradually abandoning the classics and strengthening scientific studies."

"It might have been better if he'd devoted himself to classical studies," dryly comments Claudio.

"His life, however, was not totally without tension and incidents, like when, in 1940, a lacrosse match between Harvard and Annapolis Navy cadets was interrupted by the cadets' coach because a black student was playing on the Harvard team. This event caused an immense stir, but instead of protesting against that racist gesture, Conant apologized to the commanding admiral of Annapolis for having fielded a black student on the team. Other rather embarrassing incidents were sparked by a series of meetings with high-ranking Nazi officials, the most infamous being the invitation given to Ernst Hanfstaengl to attend the opening of summer courses at Harvard. This brilliant former student with an American mother and father of ancient German nobility had become the Führer's press secretary at only twenty-five years of age. His participation in the commencement ceremony, where he gave the Nazi salute and offered a donation to fund the promotion of Germanic studies at Harvard, led to objections from the audience and articles of protest in the press. In those years, because of this climate, there was a decrease in the enrollment of students of Jewish origin."

"But did he have Nazi sympathies or not?" asks Claudio.

"For a while Conant thought that the conflict in Europe pitted communism against anti-communism and that the only choice was to support the anti-communist front. So in this sense, he was in favor of fascism and Nazism, even if the motivation given by President F. D. Roosevelt to justify intervention also played on the opposition between free and democratic countries on the one hand and dictatorial countries on the other. Whatever his personal vision of Germany, it should be said that, once his country decided to intervene in the war, Conant strongly supported that decision, and became a staunch interventionist. Then, during the Second World War, by participating in the 'Century Group' (an informal group of very powerful interventionists) and then founding the National Defense Research Committee (NDRC), he created a cast iron network of political support and protection around him. As Chairman of the NDRC, he played a leading role in initiating the 'Manhattan Project' for the production of the first nuclear bomb, and played other equally important roles in all subsequent military projects, so much so that he was known as the 'War Administrator.' After the Second World War, he became a board member of the National Foundation of Science and of the Atomic Energy Commission, covering the roles High Commissioner and U.S. Ambassador to Germany from 1953 to 1957. In other words, definitely an important person but also very controversial."

"Your research is brilliant, but I found it horribly depressing. It seems that the more intelligent a person is, the more perverse are the instruments of death he can develop. Contamination of the ground and air affects both civilians and the two armies, without discrimination, and then it continues to damage future generations. What's the sense in occupying or liberating a country if the price you pay is the creation of generations of mutilated people? They all seem crazy to me."

Chapter Twelve

THE RUSSELL-EINSTEIN
MANIFESTO

*"If the radiance of a thousand suns were to burst
into the sky that would be like the splendor of
the Mighty One" ... and "I am become Death, the
shatterer of worlds."*

–Bhagavad Gita

"Even if the research that I have found," says Claudio as he begins addressing his newsroom colleagues, "has more to do with history than with current events, I would like to spend a couple of minutes showing it to you, because, unlike the Groves report, this has given me a little hope. Listen to this: 'In view of the fact that in any future world war, nuclear weapons will certainly be employed, and that such weapons threaten the continued existence of mankind, we urge the governments of the world to realize, and to acknowledge publicly, that their purpose cannot be furthered by a world war, and we urge them, consequently, to find peaceful means for the settlement of all matters of dispute between them.'"[32]

"Ohhh, about time! Who's the noble soul?" asks Amba.

"Noble souls, actually. The letter is known as the 'Russell-Einstein' manifesto, but it was signed by thirteen Nobel laureates, the others being Max Born, Percy W. Bridgman, Leopold Infeld, Frédéric Joliot-Curie, Herman J. Muller, Linus Pauling, Cecil F. Powell, Joseph Rotblat and Hideki

Yukawa. I'll read you another piece: 'We appeal as human beings to human beings: Remember your humanity, and forget the rest. If you can do so, the way lies open to a new Paradise; if you cannot, there lies before you the risk of universal death.'"

"Very brave," comments Amba.

"This manifesto was published in 1955. It's an extraordinary text, with no ideological pretext or cultural presumption, a document that sprang from an awareness that there was no turning back from the chosen path, the path of nuclear supremacy.

"1955 and 1956 were two of the worst cold war years. At that time, both superpowers, the United States and the Soviet Union, were carrying out numerous experiments aimed at studying the effect of nuclear weapons on the battlefield. For this purpose, tens of thousands of soldiers were deployed in the vicinity of bomb explosions, which caused large numbers of them to die over the following years. Meanwhile, the first fleets of nuclear powered submarines were launched, equipped with nuclear weapons. In July 1956, after Egypt announced the nationalization of the Suez Canal, it was attacked by Britain, France and Israel. They thought that this would force Egypt to give the canal back to its former owners. President Nasser responded by sinking all of the forty ships that were in the canal at that time, thus blocking it right up until 1957. Russia reacted by invading Hungary, defeating the anti-Soviet movements and occupying it with military force.

"The Kremlin then threatened to intervene on Egypt's side and launch attacks with 'all kinds of modern weapons of mass destruction' in other words H-bombs, on London and Paris. The United States, on the other hand, threatened to sell the American sterling reserves and so forced England and France to declare a cease-fire. On that occasion, the UN created its first 'peacekeeping' mission which was sent to the Suez Canal area to 'keep the borders at peace while seeking a political agreement.' In short, the Russell-Einstein manifesto and the political crisis of those years changed the way in which war and international politics were conducted.

"Fear of nuclear power became another variable that had to be taken into consideration, because nuclear weapons had acquired excessive power and anyone who showed that they intended to use them would have lost the war, even if they thought they could win from a military point of view. It was obviously necessary to reduce their potency significantly. But to do this, a scientific solution had to be found that would lower the size of the critical mass which, in the early models, might have had load of as many as twenty or twenty-two kilograms of enriched uranium. Even the scientists had to start thinking small. In other words, it was both a political and scientific problem, and I think it's been resolved, even though no one seems to have realized it yet."

"Well, if things started to go badly wrong with our investigative work, we could always specialize in historical documentaries. We're really on top of things at this point."

Chapter Thirteen

A Holiday In Antibes

Antibes, September 1993.

The sun has just set and the light from the sky seems to be reflected far out over the sea. In a small temple in the middle of the park, the professor, Giuliano Preparata and Kurt Grass are having dinner with other guests, who are talking animatedly.

"Did I ever tell you the strange story about the gray cat?" asks the professor.

"No. Come on, tell us," urges Giuliano.

"This is the story: once upon a time, an Italian chef gave a gray cat to a countess and she raised it together with her white cat, in splendid isolation. Before leaving, the cook guaranteed that the cat had been sterilized, showing a certificate as proof. But not long after, the countess went looking for him in a rage and attacked him, saying:

"You lied to me: the white cat is pregnant and there's never been any other cat in my house, apart from that gray one."

"That's absolutely impossible," replied the cook. "But let me follow the gray cat anyway and I'll show you that I'm right."

The cook followed the gray cat for several days, until at a certain point he saw it climb up on a garbage can and meow until a large number of other cats arrived. The gray cat then began to "harangue" them with its caterwauling. After having watched this scene, the cook returned satisfied to the countess and said: "I've solved the mystery, the explanation is simple: when your apparatus no longer works, you can always act in an advisory capacity."

The diners crack up laughing in the light thrown over the table by the candles, but Grass and Preparato seem to glance furtively at one another, without even smiling. A glance that needs no explanation.

After dinner, the two men stop to enjoy a last drink before going back to the villa.

"Did you understand his message, too?" asks Grass.

"Yes. In his usual ironic fashion, he told us what he's decided: "Since I can no longer do research, I'll just have to work as a consultant," answers Preparata.

"So he's decided to stop working for the company that's funding him?"

"Look around and you'll understand why. Yesterday he explained to me that he can charge the rent for this wonderful villa and its park to the company's expense account, and feed fifty people lunch and dinner for a whole month, but he can't spend a penny on the laboratory without presenting an official request accompanied by detailed studies, estimates and working plans."

"These six weeks have been really intense. As a theoretical physicist, I find it very interesting to speculate on a series of concepts that still have to be perfected, so that I can understand the phenomenon of so-called "cold fusion," these "coherent states of matter" so to speak. But this villa is a gilded cage, where you can live like a lord fluttering here and there, just as long as you do nothing. And there are always bars that will stop you from actually flying away."

"I think you're right, but personally I don't have sufficient information to understand his choice."

"I think it has to do with some secret that we know nothing about. I've heard a lot of talk in American circles about the possibility of replacing palladium with uranium, which obviously has military implications. And that possibility might alarm the sponsors, who would therefore want to control the research very closely. It makes me think that a crucial moment has been reached: either you choose to work for some military facility, or you try to focus, as we do, on the industrial potential of this discovery. This research area is increasingly complex and there's one particular detail that I simply can't understand: the attitude of the people proposing to fund this research has some mysterious aspects, which leaves you constantly expecting some surprise."

Chapter Fourteen

Percy Williams Bridgman and His Forgotten Discovery

The feeling of understanding is as private as the feeling of pain. The act of understanding is at the heart of all scientific activity; without it any ostensibly scientific activity is as sterile as that of a high school student substituting numbers into a formula. For this reason, science, when I push the analysis back as far as I can, must be private.

–Percy William Bridgman

"Today it's my turn to report and I'd like a bit of silence," begins Diesel.

"Come on then, go ahead," Claudio urges him.

"I started with a PowerPoint presentation on the weapons used in the latest conflicts, in which the Bridgman effect was mentioned, and I tried to understand what it was talking about. Even though there was a gap of more than fifty years, I managed to find an article published in the Physical Review of November 1935, signed by that very same Percy Williams Bridgman, Nobel Prize for Physics, also known for his work *The Logic of Modern Physics*, and one of the leading world experts on the physics of high pressures."

"Strange that there should be such a gap in this sort of publication, given that he's a Nobel laureate..." comments Amba.

"There is an explanation and you'll hear it in a moment. That article stated that there's a critical threshold of pressure beyond which solid matter is pulverized and ionizing radiation and fast particles are emitted. In that article he described what happened to a sample of metal subjected to 50,000 atmospheres and simultaneously subjected to shear stress. Well, there's always a critical value which varies from substance to substance, which once exceeded determines the explosion of the sample, not through vaporization but by producing particles on the order of a micron, as well as a whole range of paranuclear phenomena. Matter is pulverized and organized into these micro-domains. You can find more complete discussion of the topic in the book The *Physics of High Pressure* published in 1947."

"Could this be the phenomenon that makes depleted uranium explode in a cloud of micro-particles when it hits the armor of a tank, freeing up energy that can disassemble the binding energy of uranium 235?" asks Amba.

"I thought about that too. Even if I don't know how many atmospheres are needed to go beyond the critical threshold of depleted uranium, and if I accept the order of 50,000 atmospheres, stated by several sources, we can hypothesize that the disintegration of a uranium projectile is determined by the Bridgman effect, since the pressure produced by today's shaped charge warheads, thanks to the particular concave mirror form placed at the base of the projectile tip, is in the order of millions of atmospheres."

"But how did Bridgman explain this phenomenon?" queries Amba.

"Bridgman didn't give any explanation of his discovery. In a normal situation, it would have created a lot of attention, with debates and opposing hypotheses, and yet nothing of that kind happened. After the article in 1935 and the book in 1947, which could certainly not have gone unnoticed, nothing, there's no mention of the topic, neither criticism nor praise, just complete silence.

"Bridgman received the Nobel Prize in 1946 for his studies with high pressures. Even though he was retiring by nature, he met the best scientists of that century through his work, like Albert Einstein, who suggested he use quantum physics to try and explain the amazing results of his research. The scientist was a close friend of Conant, the president of Harvard University, where he also taught. We also know that he met J. Robert Oppenheimer and that Henry Kissinger was one of his students on a summer course.

"In August 1961, Percy Williams Bridgman shot himself in the head in his mountain home, at the age of 79. By then he was in the last stages of bone cancer which had spread throughout his body, and he left these notes which stand as a manifesto for euthanasia: 'It isn't decent for society to make a man do this thing himself. Probably this is the last day I will be able to do it myself.'

"After a few years, it became known that the military was continuing to do research precisely on Bridgman's discovery, cataloged under the acronym S.B.E.R, i.e. 'Structure Breaking Energy Release,' and it seems this research is being carried out in both Russian and American military laboratories. So the Bridgman effect is apparently the basis for the production of a new type of weapon."

"For those who see military science as pure destruction, there's nothing strange about that," says Amba. "Matter is disintegrated, it's perfectly normal that there's this show of interest. The silence of the scientific research community, both academic and private, about these findings, can however raise questions about their real autonomy. It may mean that the military can specify which topics should be censored in scientific research, and civil research seems ready to toe the line without any objection whatsoever."

"I like Bridgman," concludes Sci. "First of all, he signed the Russell-Einstein manifesto against the use of the H-bomb. I respect the way he chose to die, a scientist who was different from the others."

Chapter Fifteen

ENRICHED URANIUM
IN KHIAM

The investigative newsroom works somewhat differently from other newsrooms where eyes must be focused on the constant flow of news from agencies and nothing can be overlooked. The investigative newsroom instead has to search for news which, because of its significance or complexity, needs to be explored in depth. Some tasks, like monitoring the main foreign online newspapers from all over the world, can be done routinely every day. And it is in fact news from one of these papers that may suddenly spark the idea for an investigation.

On August 21, 2006 an English newspaper, the *Daily Star*, published in Lebanon and also distributed on the Internet, reports that: "A high concentration of non-identified radioactive materials has been found in a crater in Khiam in southern Lebanon, on the border with Israel."

The crater was created by the bombing carried out by Israel on July 25, on the thirteenth of the thirty-five days of armed conflict between Israel and Hezbollah.

Not many hours usually pass between the moment when the idea first emerges and the moment of departure. The procedure is well-tested: the passports are always ready, the visas too, the necessary vaccinations have already been done, the travel agency is in the same basement and by now its staff know the investigative journalists by name.

In Beirut, Claudio has arranged to meet Mohamed Duhar in an old café in Hamra. He is a photographer who lives in Khiam and has documented the bombing with photographs and films.

Mohamed is a man in his forties, tall, heavy-set, passionate about his work and his country, kind and generous as the people of Southern Lebanon so often are.

"After the cease-fire, I went into Khiam to film the devastation caused by the war. The first thing that struck me was the smell, very strong ... I had to put a cloth over my face because I couldn't breathe. While I was filming, I heard people warning each other not to touch the things that had been destroyed by the bombing and to keep far away from the fumes to avoid injury," recalls Duhar.

"Did anything particularly strike you about those bombings?" asks Claudio.

"Yes, there was something. I noticed it as I was re-watching the films of the bombing in Khiam. Remember that Khiam was the first town to fall into the hands of the Israelis, who built a detention and torture center there. Then it became a Hezbollah stronghold, and they turned the special prisons into a museum dedicated to the resistance. So both the Israelis and Hezbollah know the area well, the shape of the land and the existence of underground shelters. While I was studying the images, I noticed a click in the audio that came at the same time as the explosion, probably caused by magnetic turbulence. The sound of the blast arrived a few seconds later and, watching closely, you could also see that the explosion was preceded by a sort of aura that radiated all around before the flames and smoke appeared. The flare-ups then came in four stages, as if the missiles had in fact exploded four times. Perhaps it had been planned like that to penetrate and destroy the underground shelters."

"Has anyone measured the presence of radiation?"

"Yes, professor Kubka who teaches physics at the University and actually comes from Khiam. I have his phone number, if you want."

At the University of Beirut, Professor Ibrahim Kubka walks warily up to Claudio. He has the face of an intelligent and calm person, speaks quietly and always waits for the other person to finish speaking before he begins. In short, a polite and helpful person.

"The town of Khiam called me to say there was radiation," begins the professor. "They asked me for help in understanding what was happening. So I went to Khiam, which is my hometown, and I started to assess the effects of radiation on people. I spent twenty days in the war zones and the impact of missiles around me was really horrible ... for families, for children. All the roads and bridges had been destroyed by missiles, there were huge craters. I can't say what type of weapon was used."

"Can you take me to Khiam to see the areas you're talking about?"

"I can easily do that; I go back every weekend. We can go together on Friday."

The mountains in southern Lebanon bear the traces of old Crusader castles, which still appear impregnable perched on the steep rocky cliffs where they were built; as invincible as the various military posts built by the Israelis and Hezbollah on the two different sides of the border. Yet, just as those castles have outlived their purpose, so will these military outposts sooner or later lose their purpose, anachronistic and ludicrous as they are in a piece of land which since biblical times has always been a center for business and trading between different cultures

Coming up the Litani river valley, it always strikes you how little water there is in the river and yet how it manages to transform the arid and barren rocks of the surrounding mountains into a green and shady carpet. It would be a gentle landscape if it were not for the carcasses of cars and armored vehicles that still lie alongside the road, and the constant stops due to a broken bridge or a piece of road that has fallen away. The village of Khiam sits on top of a mountain.

At first sight, it seems to be completely destroyed, but ruins unexpectedly alternate with houses under construction. Professor Ibrahim Kubka seems to move easily among those ruins and, at a certain point, comes to a standstill in front of a house under construction close to another that has been destroyed.

"This large crater was caused by an Israeli shell," Kubka begins. "It created radiation waves that reached 800 nanosievert an hour, while the average that is tolerated is between 30 and 60."

"Where did this radiation come from?" asks Claudio.

"Certainly from uranium. I collected samples from this and another twenty craters, not only in Khiam, but throughout southern Lebanon. In Khiam alone, I collected samples from five craters."

"And how deep was the crater?"

"Ten meters."

"Do you think there's still something down there?"

"I think so. I think something's still hiding down there. The highest level of radiation was in the Khiam crater, but in other craters I detected radiation levels around 300-400 nanosievert. One of these craters is located in the Bekaa Valley; they told me there's a high level of radiation there, too."

"And those ruins over there ... what are they?"

"That was a UNIFIL (United Nations Interim Force In Lebanon) post. Look how thick the cement is, more than one meter. They had sent their coordinates to the Israeli army to avoid being hit, but right on July 25, shortly before the bombing that created the radioactive crater, a remote-controlled bomb killed the four UN officers inside."

"Do you think there's a connection between the UN observers being killed and this radioactive crater?"

"The connection seems obvious to me: first they killed the UN observers with a remote-controlled bomb and then the bomb that created this crater exploded. When war breaks out everything may be connected, or perhaps there is no connection whatsoever."

"Did you have any problems doing these tests?"

"There's always been some pressure, in the sense that I wasn't supposed to say anything about the radiation in Lebanon, but God made me a free person and I can't just follow orders from the authorities. They can do what they want."

"Has anybody else measured the radioactivity in the crater?"

"Yes, I went with a British researcher to do some more measurements. I can give you his contact details if you like."

Fortunately, the trip to London can be avoided. William Greenstep is connected on Skype twenty-four hours a day and with a mere phone call, Claudio can interview him by video.

"Can you tell me about the tests you did in Khiam?"

"When I went to Khiam with Dr. Kubka, we visited at least five or six different craters, but in particular the one in which we detected the most radiation. While he measured the radiation in the crater, I inspected the area around it. When I went up on the roof of a nearby house, I found pieces of earth and stone that had come from the crater."

"Were you able to analyze them?"

"I took some samples to England and discussed them with Dr. Crisby, who's the technical advisor to the UK Ministry of Defense Oversight Board on Depleted Uranium. Alan noticed that two of these samples recorded higher than normal radioactivity and he had the samples analyzed in the Harwell nuclear laboratory, one of the most authoritative research centers in the world in this field. On October 17, Harwell gave me the results of the analysis: I thought they would have found traces of depleted uranium, but it was a shock to discover that there was enriched uranium in the samples. It took me a while to understand why they had used it. Enriched uranium does not exist in nature, only in nuclear reactors. The uranium found in the crater created by the missile in Lebanon is truly amazing. The report on radiation in Khiam is extremely important because it's exactly the type of information that we feared we would find, sooner or later."

"What conclusion did you come to after these results?"

"There were two hypotheses: either a penetration bomb, like those used to hit protected targets such as underground bunkers, or else a guided bomb or missile with a uranium head... Either way, it contained enriched and not depleted uranium."

After this shocking discovery, according to the rules, both sides should be heard and, as could easily be imagined, a barrage of denials arrived. The Israeli army denied using uranium-enhanced weapons in Lebanon: "We do not employ weapons whose use is prohibited by international laws or conventions," even though these weapons cannot be prohibited precisely because they are new. The President of the Lebanese National Council for Scientific Research stated, "No radiation was found after the Israeli bombing." On November 1, however, the Lebanese government ordered some samples of soil and water to be taken from the biggest craters, to verify the possible existence of radioactive substances.

Even the UN agency for environmental protection took samples in thirty-two sites in southern Lebanon, finding only a concentration of natural uranium ten times higher than normal, though there is no natural uranium mine in this area. On November 2, the School of Ocean Sciences – another British laboratory – confirmed the results found by Harwell: there was slightly enriched uranium in the Khiam crater. William Greenstep is convinced that a new class of weapons was used in Khiam, just like in Afghanistan and Iraq.

"My research shows that Lockheed Martin obtained a patent for these high-density warheads in 1997," continues

Greenstep. "In paragraph 4 of the patent, it says that the penetrator is made of tungsten and in section 5 it talks about a depleted uranium penetrator."

"Could this be a new kind of tactical nuclear weapon?"

"If it's a tactical nuclear weapon, it certainly doesn't work through a process of nuclear fission. We can say this because we measured the spectrogram of the material and it contains no trace of gamma rays, which are caused by uranium fission. So we can exclude that at least. I'm not an expert on weapons, but I imagine a bomb works like this: inside, there's a metal rod encased in reinforced ribbing, filled with what could be called a particularly reactive metal. It's not quite clear what that is, but my guess is uranium dust ... of nanoparticles. In the rear part, there's a kind of mechanism that triggers combustion. When the bomb explodes, the particles emerge and burn, creating an area where the temperature is very high, from which an extremely high speed flash bursts out."

"Is the sample you analyzed in line with this type of weapon?"

"Absolutely."

"Is the civilian population of Israel also at risk?"

"Certainly. About a year ago, my colleague and I found a high concentration of uranium in the ventilation system of a nuclear facility 40 miles from London. The point is that all the uranium used in war doesn't just contaminate the battle fields, but spreads all over the planet, so we all risk being contaminated. And if the Israelis use uranium in Lebanon, it'll be found wherever the wind blowing from Lebanon carries it."

Chapter Sixteen

JEY WHO NEVER SLEEPS

"What time is it?" asks Claudio.

"That's the fourth time you've asked," says Diesel. "It must be half past four. Why?"

"I have to call Jey and I don't know if he'll be awake yet."

"Does he live in the United States?"

"No, in Ravenna or Ferrara."

"You don't even know where he lives ... have you met him at least?"

"Yes, but only once. He's one of our freelancers, a young guy, very smart. After that first meeting, I've only seen him on the net. He never wanted to tell me where he lived.... I only know that it's somewhere in the north. He says he doesn't want to tell me because he doesn't want to be disturbed. He's the only one in our group who can spend nine hours straight doing research on the Internet. He also knows several languages and has a phenomenal memory. All our colleagues in the newsroom are worked off their feet, so when I need research done on some complex topic, I know I can count on him. I'm waiting for the results of his research on dirty bullets. Every so often, particularly on very complicated topics, we also use him for parallel verification of our research. In this profession, it's easy to make mistakes, you're in too much of a hurry, there are too many variables, so it's useful to have someone who can do research on the same subject."

Claudio's computer suddenly chirps and burbles. Skype starts up, and Jey's face appears, a cross between Jimi Hendrix and Antonio Gramsci, with extremely loud music in the background.

"Turn off the music," Claudio urges him.

"Oh, sure. Sorry, I need it to keep me awake," says Jey. "I did everything and I found some really interesting stuff. Listen up now: January 23, 2001 a team of researchers from the Spietz laboratory, dependent on the Swiss Federal Institute of Technology, published a report commissioned by the UN on samples of depleted uranium munitions from Kosovo. In these samples they found traces of uranium 236, uranium 232 and plutonium. The first two are uranium isotopes that don't exist in nature – this shows that the uranium in question isn't depleted but comes from nuclear reactor waste materials or else a process of nuclear fission that took place right there and then. The report is signed by Max Weller and Christoph Wirtz.

"The news was first reported by the *New York Times* on January 17, 2001 in an article by Marline Simons, with some interesting interviews, like the one with Monique Sené, a French nuclear physicist, who claims: 'U236 is created in a nuclear reactor and is almost certainly produced from the waste substances of this fuel; there are no other known sources of U236.' Another American physicist, Steve Fetter, says that U236 was known to exist in depleted uranium munitions, but was not really considered dangerous, because alpha radiation doesn't penetrate into bones or bone-marrow where leukemia can develop.

"Jean-Francois Lacronique, Director of the National Radiation Protection Institute in France, expressed a different opinion, declaring that he was concerned about the discovery of U236, since it is ten times more radioactive than depleted uranium and works much faster. After an explosion, U236 becomes pulverized dust and can be inhaled, remaining radioactive for two hundred days. He also said that U236 had been found in the urine and tissues of American soldiers who took part in the first Gulf War. The particles of plutonium, americium and neptunium also found in the analyzed samples were even more dangerous.

"In more or less the same period, the book *Depleted Uranium: The Invisible War*[33] was published in France. It cites several documents from the U.S. Department of Energy which reveal it was a known fact that uranium from the Paducah facility might contain traces of neptunium and plutonium. This facility is one of the main centers for the production and storage of so-called depleted uranium. The authors note symptoms similar to those of the Gulf syndrome that have appeared among workers in the center. Two more American nuclear power plants were allegedly involved in this recycling of nuclear waste: in Portsmouth and Oak Ridge. The book was reviewed by several foreign newspapers such as the *Independent*, which stated that the Pentagon had known about the presence of traces of plutonium and U236 in depleted uranium products for at least six years. The paper also reports that the Pentagon spokesman, Kenneth Bakon, admitted this was true. It would be strange if he had denied it considering that, in 1992, the Paducah facility in Kentucky had been accused of 'fraud, pollution, abuse and mismanagement' by the General Accounting Office, the official watchdog of the United States Government. The report stated that the center recycled reactor waste without the necessary safeguards, endangering the health of workers."

"Is there anything else we should know?"

"Yes, there's an article written by Professor Samuel Cohen, an important person who took part in the Manhattan project on the nuclear bomb. He was the inventor of the so-called 'neutron bomb,' which can kill people with radiation leaving infrastructures intact. According to what he himself said, he convinced President Reagan to build seven-hundred of them. He claimed that he was awarded a medal by Pope John Paul II in 1979 for his bid to reform modern warfare by reducing its destructive effects. He worked at the

RAND Corporation, an American think tank: and he was to hire Herman Kahn, the military strategist behind the Cold War, who also theorized enhanced radiation tactical weapons. In an essay entitled 'Enhanced Radiation: Setting the Record Straight,' published in the Strategic Review, Cohen describes how so-called depleted uranium (DU) projectiles function:

> Today's most effective conventional anti-tank weapons are designed to penetrate tank armor and produce effects which will kill or disable the tank crews.... [T]he bulk of NATO's battlefield nuclear weapons (and perhaps also those of the Soviet Union) have their most extensive anti-tank effects in the form of nuclear radiation against tank crews.... During the last year, a major international debate has flared over the issue of development and deployment of enhanced radiation [ER] weapons. Misunderstanding has been rife with regard to the effects of these devices. Since the advent of nuclear weapons, a major emphasis has been on designing large-yield devices rather than "clean" low-yield and discriminating tactical nuclear weapons which could reduce unintended damage. ER weapons have the desirable advantage for NATO of making it possible to attack military targets without causing widespread structural damage. The outcry against ER tends to be based on erroneous assumptions and/or emotion. The addition of more discriminating weapons including ER weapons to the NATO arsenal will be a step towards a more credible tactical nuclear posture for the Alliance...

"Professor Cohen also invented a most insidious trap designed to flush out any prospective buyers of nuclear weapons, through the announcement that there was a substance, so-called 'red mercury,' a non-existent element which, subverting all the concepts known to theoretical physics, could be used to trigger the explosion of a nuclear weapon with no need for critical mass. Cohen claimed that it was produced by the Russians and that terrorists would soon acquire it.

"It would apparently serve as bait to catch ignorant terrorists seeking weapons of mass destruction, but after having successfully experimented with the ignorance and confusion of public opinion on nuclear power, it'd probably have been a perfect excuse to increase fear and legitimize any action against the so-called 'rogue states.' Cohen in fact supported the theory that Saddam possessed weapons of mass destruction and, according to his information, had fifty red mercury bombs."

"Jey, you were great as usual, thanks."

As they disconnect "Sympathy for the Devil" returns to peak volume. "Just call when you need me."

Chapter Seventeen

A Dinner According to the Book

After a particularly complex investigation is broadcast, the newsroom becomes the crossroads for hundreds of facts that the most disparate people are interested in getting aired: a load of enthusiastic calls on the group of ENEA scientists, some controversy on the subject of cold fusion, further information from many Middle Eastern editors alarmed by the radioactivity in the Khiam crater. The delicate decision to choose which calls should be passed on, and which quickly written down, is made by the editorial assistants, two very bright girls coming from the most radical, hi-tech underground. In comparison to them, the five journalists are first-grade schoolchildren: there is no technological task, no sophisticated research, no breathtaking film editing, no news items buried beneath millions of others, they cannot unearth.

They are the ones who direct the traffic. And one of them is contacted on Skype by William Greenstep. The call is immediately transferred onto Claudio's computer.

"Good morning, Claudio. I have some news for you," begins Greenstep. "When I was in Beirut in September, I asked to visit the southern part of the city. A guide took me to visit what one might call Hezbollah's 'reception center.'"

"It was in an area called Haret Hreyk, the most heavily bombed zone ... I saw three damaged ambulances there, so I asked if I could take the air filter from one of them and

I had it analyzed. They've just brought me the results: it contains enriched uranium. It belonged to a vehicle that had only been in the war for fourteen days. So all the enriched uranium inside it accumulated in only two weeks. I'd advise you to look into this story."

"I was thinking about going back to the Lebanon, to follow up on the developments with the Khiam bomb, so I could try to film the ambulance," replies Claudio.

"I'll give you all the contacts you need. My guess is that they used the same type of bomb in South Beirut as the one dropped on Khiam. What's more, I think that they habitually drop at least two different bombs so that the enriched uranium radioactivity is disguised: one bomb with enriched uranium and another with non-depleted uranium. The use of non-depleted uranium – natural, in other words – is important because it makes it extremely difficult for laboratories to identify enriched uranium. In fact, when non-depleted uranium burns and turns to ash, it cannot be distinguished from so-called background radiation from natural sources. It is in fact this aspect that, for five years, has allowed American and British governments and military forces – and even the UNEP (United Nations Environmental Program) – to say that uranium weapons were not a problem, everything was put down to high background radioactivity..."

Claudio is due to leave the following day, but there's time for another small event that upsets the atmosphere in the newsroom: a call from Norma, the woman who had also been at the conference on new weapons in Florence. The assistants receiving the phone calls who are blessed with more insight than their journalist colleagues, have already realized that this call leads to a dead end – coining an expression in their personal code: Hans Christian Andersen, which stands for Little Match Girl, in other words "cock teaser" – but they cannot resist passing on the call to Claudio, whose tone of voice immediately betrays a certain excitement, "Hi gorgeous, you won't believe it but I was just thinking about you ... how nice to hear from you ... I'm leaving for Beirut tomorrow, but we could have dinner together this evening ... if you like ... let's say nine? Yes, I'll pick you up."

No sooner does he put down the phone than he notices the sudden silence of the entire editorial staff and all eyes fixed on him. He immediately realizes that he has made a mistake ... an incredibly serious error. There is an implicit code of behavior in the newsroom, which above all asserts that people should not flaunt the fact that they are about to leave. Journalists even try to avoid saying where they are going, especially to people outside the newsroom, and not only for security reasons, but also from respect for those colleagues who would themselves like to have the opportunity. Acting like a great reporter on the lines of Hemingway and spreading the word about their journeys is not part of the investigative newsroom's genetic makeup, quite the reverse. They take pride in coming back when the reporters from other newsrooms are just arriving in the field, and vice versa.

Television is crammed with journalists who just love to be present at all the major tragedies in the world and are expert at parroting the most banal of clichés; their face in the foreground and, way in the background, the crowd or dead bodies or tanks. Those who work with the investigation team do not put their face in the foreground, they look for motives, reasons why, this is the story they want to tell.

Apologizing now would just worsen the situation. The damage has been done and the silence is getting heavy. For Claudio, the evening has started badly.

Most human beings are dominated by a kind of experiential frenzy, thanks to which any attractive proposal that is offered even at the worst moment, has a good chance of receiving enthusiastic support. This is what Claudio is thinking as, just home from work, he has to carve up the forty minutes that separate him from the appointment with Norma between the choice of clothing for the trip and preparation for the scenario that may present itself at the end of the evening: my place or yours?

In any case, his flight leaves at 9:30 A.M. for Beirut.

Claudio is always ready for any eventuality, but this time there are just too many: the suit, the shirt for dinner, tidying up the apartment for a possible continuation of the evening. His thoughts begin to overlap chaotically in his mind.

His hands are full of objects and he must get a move on: he unthinkingly puts the Bulgari perfume in his bag for Beirut and a packet of Lactobacillus, his faithful helper in times of gastric difficulty, in that evening's jacket; the evening's shirt and cufflinks with the clothes in his traveling backpack and the "self-ironing" shirt, as gray as all the roads in the world, laid out among the evening clothes.

In the end he shows up for the date in a freshly ironed black suit, perhaps just slightly deformed by the vials of Lactobacillus in his pockets, with a virtually imperishable, cement-gray shirt, all worn under a daringly red Goretex windbreaker, with indestructible black builder's boots on his feet. Norma, on the other hand, is dressed to kill: Six inch heels, thigh highs, black leather mini skirt and jacket covering a low-cut pink silk shirt. Blond feathery hair framing her face. Claudio waves to her from the other side of the street, but she does not notice him, or perhaps does not recognize him, and starts talking to a young man who is going towards the same restaurant, then takes his arm and goes in with him. Claudio catches up with them and cannot grasp if the third person is unexpected or deliberate. So, to show he is above all this, he begins an intense conversation with the stranger on the pros and cons of the mobile phone that the man is fiddling with.

"An excellent phone, even if it has low screen resolution ... barely average brightness and the integration of different programs doesn't allow you to cut and paste."

"Don't worry. It's my phone, not yours ..."

"These are objective technical evaluations. It seems excessively heavy compared to the previous model and its battery life is not sufficiently ..."

Without giving him time to finish the sentence, the unwelcome guest decides to abandon ship. "Well, I'll leave you two alone now. Talk to you soon Norma."

"I'll call you tomorrow afternoon, perhaps we can have dinner together in the evening."

"Who's that guy?"

"He's my editor."

"Do you often have dinner together?"

"When it happens."

"Is there something going on between you?"

"That, if you don't mind, is my business,. But let's talk about your work: what's cooking?"

"I think I've got hold of a good story, but it's rather long and complicated and develops over twenty years."

"And how long have you got to tell it?"

"A little over twenty minutes."

"That's great! Give me the gist."

"It's to do with the falsification of certain terms, the hiding of a discovery and a criminal war strategy."

"Explain."

"The falsification of terms lies in the fact that what we call depleted uranium shells are actually projectiles made of waste radioactive products from nuclear reactors."

"The hidden discovery?"

"The process of cold fusion, if applied to uranium, allows a nuclear process to be triggered without fissile material."

"And the criminal war strategy?"

"The use of dirty uranium to pollute and decimate enemy populations for generations to come."

"Do you think I could write an article with your help?"

"I really don't think so, we still have to get confirmation and collect data."

"Is that why you're going to Beirut?"

"Yes, that too."

"'Scuse me, I've just seen Guido, a colleague. Wait a moment, I'll say hello and come straight back."

Norma walks away and after a few minutes the waiter arrives.

Claudio, tired of waiting, orders a bottle of Gewurztraminer and a seafood salad for two. Norma does not come back for a quarter of an hour, returning just as the waiter is serving the two starters.

"Who ordered this? I hate seafood salad. You can just take mine back, thanks. What were you saying about uranium?"

"If you charge uranium with deuterium ..."

"With what?"

"Do you know about deuterium?"

"No. Can't you make it a little easier? I don't understand you, Claudio. Look, you're a good journalist but too complicated. You bore me ... I don't understand what you're talking about ..."

"Go on Wikipedia and try to understand what deuterium is..."

"Why don't you go on Wikipedia! What's up with you anyway? We go out to dinner together, I turn down two other invitations and all you do is talk about deuterium. Not one question about my work, or how I'm doing ... and if I ask you to help me write a piece on your ravings, you don't even want to do it."

"Norma don't do this, you're just so beautiful this evening and you're embarrassing me ..." says Claudio, taking her hand.

"Don't pull those calf eyes at me ... it's either deuterium or calf's eyes ... no middle road ... and anyway, you're like all the others, you just want to fuck. The only difference is that you try it on with the excuse of deuterium, while the others at least say something more credible."

"We can change the subject if you like. I'll talk about the misunderstandings related to the God particle."

"Don't be so vulgar. That's enough! I'd rather go to my friends' table. Our dinner ends here. Good night."

"But there really is a God particle. It's called the Higgs boson, too."

"I already know what particle you're talking about ... you're disgusting," and with these words, she gets up and leaves.

Chapter Eighteen

ENRICHED URANIUM
IN BEIRUT

Claudio is smiling as he comes out of the restaurant. When things do not go right, he can never refrain from smiling as he thinks about the irony of the situation. He had not excluded the possibility of a short "hot fusion" with Norma but he had only managed to talk to her about the mechanisms of cold fusion – all in all, he had not foreseen such an ending to the evening, and anyway, tomorrow he had that meeting with a Hezbollah spokesperson.

As Claudio's plane lands in Beirut, the two editorial assistants in the newsroom have already reconstructed the events of the previous evening, without anyone needing to inform them: "He probably talked about deuterium and she, totally out of her depth, and trying to avoid a nuclear explosion that has no part in a cockteaser's plans, undoubtedly left with one of her colleagues."

Beirut has an appeal similar to that of New York: by merely crossing a street, you can go from a wealthy neighborhood to a poor one, from one religion to another, from customs and rules of one kind to totally different ones. It is not simple to enter the Shiite area of Beirut controlled by Hezbollah fighters, particularly after the ruins and suffering caused by the war.

During the meeting with Hezbollah's press officer, Claudio tries to get permission to film the ambulance mentioned by GreenStep in his phone call, but there seems to be no trace of the vehicle. By way of reply, the organization's representative begins to ask him numerous questions about his work and the reasons for his visit, plainly concerned when he hears Claudio talking about the threat of radioactivity. And it is easy to understand why: the news could easily create panic, causing a mass exodus. At the same time, it might cause even worse problems if they do not give this information. The discussion goes on until it is nearly sunset, and when Claudio realizes that there is not enough light left to film, he resolutely demands an answer, whatever it is. After a long silence, the Hezbollah spokesperson, with an unexpected smile, replies, "You're a good person, we'll take you to the ambulance."

The light is terrible and Claudio tries to do miracles with the limited possibilities of his small camera. He also manages to meet the driver of the ambulance, interviewing him right then and there. This is how he describes the events:

> Ambulances are usually driven by groups of several people. There were three of us driving this one. It was used mainly in Beirut, in the bombed area, specifically in the Haredge zone. Sometimes we went in even during the bombing, in the midst of smoke and dust, to help victims in the southern area of Beirut. I think this ambulance had been moved to fifty or seventy different places since the beginning of the attack on July 12. There were almost daily bombings and usually the ambulance just arrived where it could, because the roads had been wiped out. We went into the zones that had been hit and often collected only tattered shreds of the victims. The ambulance only went once to the south of Lebanon, to Tyre, when it was transporting medicinal drugs. After a few days, on its way back, it was hit during a bomb attack.

As always, a knot of people has formed around Claudio. Among them there is also the photographer from the

Lebanese daily newspaper, *As-Safir*, who agrees to give a short interview. "About seventeen days after the beginning of the attack, I was in Haredge, on the southern outskirts of Beirut, when a bomb exploded just two blocks away ... The shape formed by the smoke after the explosion reminded me of Hiroshima. I couldn't breathe for a few seconds. And you never get over this feeling. I don't know if it's due to the explosion or something else. But every so often, even now, I can't breathe and I start to have convulsions."

That same evening, Claudio calls Greenstep via Skype from an Internet point in the Hamra neighborhood. "It's easy to calculate how much uranium there was in the air," asserts Greenstep. "Let's consider that the ambulance had a capacity of four hundred horse power and worked for eight hours a day for more than two weeks. The concentration of uranium that we found in the filter is truly remarkable. There will probably be the same concentration in the lungs of the people who were in those areas."

"Have you heard anything about the United Nations' analyses on those samples from Khiam?" asks Claudio.

"We have two "twin samples." We took one to Harwell, the lab that works with the UK Ministry of Defense. The other was analyzed by UNEP (the United Nations Environment Program). And if UNEP were to have different results from ours, that'd be a big problem."

"Did you find enriched uranium in the water sample?"

"Enriched uranium was indeed found in ours. And UNEP should find traces, too."

"From a confidential source, it appears that, once again, the Swiss scientists in Spiez have not confirmed the analyses made in Harwell. Where the British found enriched uranium, the scientific consultants for UNEP have found only natural uranium."

"I've never appreciated the work done by UNEP. They always try to minimize the evidence showing the presence of uranium. They already did it in the Balkans. I was in

Kosovo with the Japanese TV and I measured the presence of uranium in the field while UNEP stated that there was no trace. Now everyone agrees that there really was uranium there. Everything would be so much simpler if there was no enriched uranium there ... it seems really strange to me, too, that someone should use enriched uranium, unless they aim to create a special new weapon. Why else would they use it? It's like wanting to kill the enemy by firing diamonds at them ... but the problem can't be eliminated merely by changing the data, and the presence of enriched uranium is definitely a problem, too. The most likely hypothesis is that two different bombs were used because, faced with the scientific data, there's not much doubt. If a piece of earth, taken from a war zone, is put into a machine designed to measure infinitesimal quantities of matter ... and a machine is only a machine ... it's accurate, it can't lie ... then you push a button and it tells you that there is enriched uranium in that sample ... just like the air filter and the water.... Then, as far as I'm concerned, that's the end of the story – there is definitely enriched uranium in southern Lebanon."

Walking back to his hotel in Hamra, Claudio is surprised by one particular aspect of Beirut – despite the continuous bombing and more than a thousand deaths, and the many cultures and religions, the city continues to stay alive and convey a feeling of ceaseless activity, and vibrant noise. He realizes that he is not at all afraid to go through the Hamra district at night: there are always taxis, announcing their presence with a discreet beep of their horns, or someone who as they walk past, greets him with that noblest of civic virtues, hospitality.

Before leaving, Claudio again meets professor Kubka who, with some concern, mentions the fear that has spread throughout the population of southern Lebanon after the news of radioactivity in Khiam. He also talks about Hezbollah's reluctance to consider the risks associated with this type of pollution. Even though Kubka is just now returning from Khiam, he also insists on considering less dramatic hypotheses, talking of incorrect results given by the laboratories, margins of error in the measurements. But then, in the end, with an urge for serenity, compelled by irrepressible honesty, he confides that he has analyzed the urine of some residents in the area and confirms that, in at least one case, he has found the presence of enriched uranium. He invites Claudio to spend an afternoon with him in Khiam before he leaves and Claudio willingly accepts. There, he meets the town's mayor who gives his point of view.

"The population is scared. The people who live near the crater are afraid to approach it. But many are even afraid to come into the city. Two weeks ago, a fourteen-year old girl died and many people have spoken about the mystery of her death ... but for now we can neither confirm nor deny because we don't want to increase this climate of terror. Israel has dared to create an environmental catastrophe that is causing much concern among the population. But our aquifers are connected to the Israeli ones and if experts were to confirm contamination of our groundwater, sooner or later it would happen to them, too. We ask the scientific organizations to answer this simple question: what should we do? People ask us this all the time and we must be able to give a definitive answer."

Chapter Nineteen

SOME THINGS CANNOT BE ASKED AT THE FIRST QUESTION

There are some issues that cannot be touched upon in the first question during an interview. For at least two reasons: firstly, because there would be no answer, and then because any eventual answer would probably not be understood by the person who asked the question. Often you just have to wait and in time that question slowly emerges, or occasionally the answer is spontaneously volunteered.

Journeys, movements, appointments, delays, phone calls, are all just devices that cause meetings to coincide with that temporal window in which two people talk to one another. Just as two different types of mechanics exist in physics – Newtonian and quantum – the same kinds of mechanics also exist in the lives of human beings. One that regulates the lighting up of traffic lights on the streets, the answering of telephone calls, the opening of elevators, the requests at the bar and purchases at newspaper stands; and another, more profound, which is based on two independent variables that may give unpredictable results, a sort of "quantum mechanics" of human communication that is based on a principle of indeterminacy. If you receive the impulse, you don't understand the position and vice versa. In this form of mechanics, which is the one that governs profound relationships between people, it is resignation, tiredness, movement, which make possible a random moment that frees energy, during which communication occurs between two people.

With these thoughts in mind, Claudio climbs the subway stairs, walks along sidewalks and then passageways, and eventually finds himself in a small office in front of a person who he must ask yet another question.

"Professor, we collected some information from eyewitnesses in the Lebanon that we consider to be incomprehensible," begins Claudio. "The people we interviewed told us about bombs that caused a feeling of suffocation. And then, craters were found with traces of enriched uranium but no presence of gamma irradiation residues. How can we interpret this information? Can you help us to understand it?"

"Do you remember that I asked you a question, the last time we met?" Grass then asks Claudio. "What would happen if, instead of charging palladium with deuterium, we were to charge it with uranium? This is not a question I asked by mere chance: reading the transcript of the report made by Professor Fleischmann at the tenth international conference on cold fusion, I found some important statements in a note. With regard to the so-called cold explosions observed by Bridgman in the Thirties, he wrote that 'Intense compression and shear of lattices can lead to their fragmentation into small particles in which the high energy of the initial system is converted into kinetic energy of the fragments. We believed (and still believe) that this is a process which can only be explained by Q.E.D.' Then, a little further on, he adds: 'Furthermore, we knew that the absorption of hydrogen isotopes can lead to a similar fragmentation.'

"Could you explain it more simply? Because what you said doesn't make much sense to me ..."

"As you may have noticed, Fleischmann refers to quantum mechanics, i.e. the kind of mechanics needed to explain nuclear phenomena. And it is precisely that time clause – 'We believed (and still believe) ...' – that allows us to understand his message. In simple words, he's saying: 'When I ventured into the study of these phenomena, I knew perfectly well that I was inquiring about a *nuclear process* with all that it implies. And if I did so, making public my information, it's because I thought that, in this way, I could limit the risks connected to these topics, like cold fusion, on which military secrecy is imposed.' But he says other things too. He says: 'We knew that the absorption of hydrogen isotopes can lead to a similar fragmentation.' In other words, that uranium charged with deuterium can trigger a nuclear process. Can you follow me properly? I'm skipping some steps but ... keep following me: the fragmentation of metal and the release of energy that Bridgman discovered through his experiments on compression and shear of metals, can now be obtained by charging uranium with deuterium almost to the critical threshold. Any electrical or mechanical stimulation (for example, the compression resulting from an explosion) goes beyond the threshold and triggers the cold fusion process.

"For a very short time, the energy produced in this way takes on the form of an electromagnetic field with a frequency which falls within the order of gamma rays, and which can therefore induce fission of the nuclei that make up the crystal lattice of the metal. Now, if the metal used is palladium, fission doesn't release energy and so it isn't relevant from the military point of view.

"And the facts prove it: in fact, the palladium cathodes used in the experiments at Frascati were then examined by the University of Beijing (34), who found that 10% of their nuclei had become nickel, whose atomic number, as we know, is roughly half the atomic number of the palladium nucleus. This means that during the cold fusion process, there was palladium fission. But what would have happened if there had been uranium, instead of palladium? A piece of uranium, charged with deuterium just below the critical threshold and fired at a target, may start a process of cold fusion which gives rise to an electromagnetic field with the frequency of gamma rays. This in turn produces fission of the uranium nuclei, which, unlike the palladium nuclei, make a wonderful 'nuclear bang,' with no need for fissile material, unlike the fission induced by neutrons. So then I can even explode milligrams of uranium in a nuclear way.

"In short, he eliminated the problem of fissile material, so now 'nuclear bombs the size of a bullet' can be created using the loading of deuterium as a trigger. Not only – their power can even be calibrated in such a way that they destroy a building or an underground shelter. Where do you think the radioactive uranium in Khiam comes from? And why was the United Nations look-out post destroyed before the bomb was used? Do you have any idea at all of how many tons of TNT you'd need to blow up in order to get a similar blast?

"A conventional nuclear bomb, like the ones dropped on Hiroshima and Nagasaki, had an explosive power corresponding to approximately 20,000 tons of TNT, i.e. 20 kilotons. According to expert opinion, the critical mass should be around 7-8 kilograms of U235, which is about 0.7% of natural uranium. In the conventional nuclear bomb, the charge had to be composed almost entirely of U235, so the uranium used had to be highly enriched (more than 90%). In conventional explosions, the explosive power was obtained through the fission of a small percentage of nuclei, because the explosion pulverized the part that had still not undergone fission and scattered it, thereby interrupting the phenomenon. Knowing how much energy was released by the fission of a single nucleus, the power generated by a conventional nuclear bomb corresponded to approximately 1% of fissioned nuclei. In the case of the new type of fission which we're talking about, it's not necessary to use highly enriched uranium, because the physical mechanism is not the fission of U235 nuclei due to neutrons but a different kind of rupture of nuclei due to the tremendous shaking of the material induced by another and more efficient nuclear reaction

"In conclusion, if a conventional bomb released 20 kilotons using 7-8 kg of U235 – corresponding to 1000 kilograms of natural uranium – for equal efficiency, the new fission, which is independent of the critical mass, requires only 100 grams of natural uranium to produce the explosive power of two tons of TNT. And of course, performance 'improves' when a little enriched uranium is used. Nuclear weapons can also be produced for the infantry, considering that one sole gram of natural uranium provides an explosive power equal to 20 kilograms of TNT. It's like saying that a gunshot has the same effect as a cannon.

"Do you know why the issue of nuclear weapons is no longer tackled in public? Why should they confess that they have already used them, despite the Non-Proliferation Treaty? Why should they admit that their market is booming? Today's interest in the construction of new generation nuclear power plants may also be linked to the convenience of having enriched uranium available, which would allow the efficiency of the bullets we have just mentioned to be increased. The market for 'nuclear bullets' would begin to take off.

"But you'll see, they'll give them a new name ... they'll call them 'sustainable', 'green', 'impoverished' ... all terms that you journalists use so willingly. You should never believe in the adjectives used in military terminology, like 'surgical', 'precise' or 'peaceful' ..."

"I'm following you, and what you're saying is very interesting ... but if I wanted to repeat it in a television documentary, I wouldn't know where to begin. If I tried to talk about the things you're telling me, I'd stop dead at the first objection. For example, what kind of hypothesis can we make about the enriched uranium found in Khiam?"

"Well, assuming that the measurement is correct and that enriched uranium is present in Khiam, there are two possibilities: either the bullet was formed from uranium that had already been enriched beforehand, or else the uranium became enriched due to the explosion – in other words, we'd be faced with a nuclear-type phenomenon that until now has never been used. In the first case, on the other hand, one assumes that the manufacturers of the projectile used enriched uranium. This process, which is undoubtedly very expensive, could be justified by the improved nuclear performance of the bullet. In both cases, however, the presence of enriched uranium would indicate that a nuclear phenomenon had occurred on the spot. One could argue that enriched uranium comes from nuclear waste produced by power plants, but this objection would justify the presence of radioactivity, since uranium waste from nuclear power plants is more radioactive than natural uranium. But it would be very dangerous for those handling it, i.e. manual laborers, warehouse workers and the military in the field."

"Assuming this really happened, what kind of nuclear phenomenon might it have been?"

"It's hard to say. Clearly it's not a phenomenon like the one occurring with the Hiroshima-type bombs, because those bombs needed fissile material consisting mostly of U235. So I think the most probably hypothesis is exactly the one that sounds most like science fiction."

"Chris Busby, the British researcher, told us that since we found no gamma rays or cesium-137, there can't have been a nuclear reaction."

"And what does he know about it? It wasn't a Hiroshima-type nuclear reaction. It wasn't initiated by neutrons, but not only neutrons exist, after all. As a hypothesis, if the electromagnetic field that was produced had had the frequency of gamma rays, it would have been able to split the nuclei differently from the ways that we know about."

"So it could be a different kind of phenomenon. We could envisage a kind of bomb with two stages: one chemical, the other nuclear..."

"Many things can be envisaged. When you're dealing with phenomena of this type, you have to be fairly open minded, a maverick, and not believe that the present is just a repetition of the past. We might also find ourselves face to face with the military use of natural phenomena that have only recently been discovered. So I'd like to suggest that anyone involved in investigating the debris left by mysterious weapons does not take for granted that every nuclear phenomenon must necessarily be like the one in Hiroshima."

"This is actually a bomb that may kill using the vast amount of energy released in an instant, rather than nuclear radiation ..."

"I'm going to make a sheer hypothesis, that may have nothing to do with what actually happened. If the core, instead of being struck by a neutron and then randomly splitting, had started to vibrate due to the electromagnetic field, then the "shell" or subnuclear structure would have been separated by the vibration and the fission fragments would not have been radioactive. This means that, after the explosion, the radioactivity would have been lower than when ordinary fission bombs are used.

"On the other hand, from the statements made by politicians and the military, we know that the great powers have mini nuclear weapons, 'mini-nukes' as President Bush called them. But if these mini nuclear weapons exist, it means that the problem of *critical mass*, a problem that is unavoidable when dealing with neutron-induced nuclear fission, has somehow been surmounted."

"When uranium projectiles impact, could they cause pulverization of the metal and, therefore, micro-fission reactions? And how is it possible for such a high temperature to be reached – 4000 ° C, as far as I know – at the moment of impact?"

91

"All official stories about depleted uranium munitions seem to cover the development of a much more evil type of weapon, developed in great secrecy since the eighties... The best-kept military secret of the past twenty years is this concealment of a new generation of weapons that use uranium in various forms."

"That's what I think, too ... but it's not enough just to imagine it, we have to prove it. It might be useful for me to talk to Fleischmann. Could I meet him?"

"He's a very helpful person, I'll give you his number and I don't think he'll have any problem meeting you. But before you disappear, I want to give you a riddle created by Lacan: A prison director calls in three prisoners and says: 'There are five disks: three white and two black, and I'm going to stick one of these discs onto each of your backs. You can see the disk on the back of the other prisoners, but you cannot speak to one another, so you won't know the color of the disk that you have on your own back. The person who understands what color disk he has on his back will come to the door of this room and give me his answer. If he's right, I'll set him free.' And with that, he stuck a white disk on the back of each prisoner. How can this riddle be solved?"

"I'll think about it, but right now I need to set up a meeting with Fleischmann."

Chapter Twenty

THE JOURNEY TO MEET PROFESSOR MARTIN FLEISCHMANN

In the wandering life of a journalist, there is always one voyage that is made with particular devotion, with a different approach. It might be thought of as a novice's search for the wise man – the subject of a thousand tales – an almost inner path of knowledge, rather than the hunt for news. For Claudio, it is the journey to meet Professor Martin Fleischmann in his English retreat. But Claudio had not even imagined that there might be problems with the transport system in the rural areas of Britain: suddenly, the bus on which he is traveling begins to shake violently, causing him to transfer his gaze, initially immersed in the bewitching green countryside of England, to the driver's head, which seems rather too relaxed since, after a night spent drinking, every now and again he apparently drops off at the wheel, leaving the bus to travel forward along a rather haphazard line towards an unspecified point on the horizon.

As if guided by a divine hand, the driver occasionally opens his eyes and suddenly pulls hard on the steering wheel, rapidly changing direction and causing the passengers to protest loudly. At this point, Claudio tries every possible trick to keep the tired driver awake. He starts with a delicate, but persistent cough, then asks about the timetable, all the places where they stop, and the history of the area. Then he is forced to talk about himself, passing from a humble and carefully prepared interview with a famous yet subsequently unrewarded candidate for the Nobel Prize, to a loud and persistent discussion with the driver about his previous night's activities. This dialogue is received with immense appreciation by the other passengers on the bus, but above all achieves the goal of eliminating the hazardous alcohol fumes from the driver's bleary mind.

Then at last it is time to get off the bus and Claudio walks away, followed by the affectionate farewells of his nameless fellow passengers.

The professor arrives late for their appointment and, after initial pleasantries, drives Claudio to his charming cottage where his wife is waiting with their magnificent dog, an Irish setter with the delightful name of 'Mouse'. After choosing the best place for the interview, Claudio rapidly sets up his equipment and begins the interview.

"Let's start at the beginning. When did you start to work on charging heavy metals with hydrogen and its isotopes?"

"I've always been interested in this field, ever since 1947 when I was still a student. But the research studies in Utah began in 1983 or 1984."

"So that was before the Royal Navy asked you to do an experiment that aimed to charge uranium with hydrogen?"

"No, you're quite wrong. No one ever asked me to carry out experiments of that kind."

"Have you ever tried to charge uranium?"

"No, but it would obviously be interesting."

"Why?"

"Because you can obtain a much higher concentration of hydrogen with uranium. And then it can be loaded or de-loaded by varying the temperature."

"In what way is uranium different from palladium? I mean, what would happen if uranium were to be charged?"

"You get a higher concentration of deuterium compared to palladium ... but I think that's a difficult question to answer..." he responds, smiling.

"I mean, palladium is not a fissile element, whereas uranium is. How would uranium react to being charged like that?"

"The mere fact of using uranium would in itself be interesting, even if it caused no change."

"What applications might it have?"

"Erm ... I'm still thinking about an energy source ... the difficulty is that the host lattices are not very stable, they break down into powder, and in this way uranium dust charged with deuterium would be produced as it would with an energy source consisting of other metals charged with gas. It would be a system in a gaseous phase."

"So an energy source, not a military weapon."

"No ... well ... It's impossible to know without doing experiments. I imagine it would just be an energy source."

"Let's put it this way – based on your experience and knowledge of theoretical physics, do you think that uranium charging might be a technique that could produce weapons?"

"It's not clear, you'd have to do experiments with that intention."

"And you've never done any, right?"

"No, we never did. I think you'd have to inform the authorities if you were doing that kind of experiment...."

"As far as you know, is there anyone in the world who can obtain this result: charging uranium with deuterium?"

"Yes. The line of reasoning leading up to this kind of experiment is perfectly logical."

"Who and where? Do you know?"

"Anyone and anywhere."

"What possible features might a weapon constructed with deuterium-charged uranium have?"

"I don't think that this, in itself, is a very "natural" way of building a weapon, given that one cannot possibly know how this physics process might be governed."

"Is a nuclear micro-bomb conceivable?"

"Anything's possible. A system which could release a large amount of energy in a very small volume is certainly plausible."

"Would it be much smaller and easier to use than a traditional nuclear bomb? Is that possible from a theoretical point of view?"

"It's possible. God knows it's possible! But there might be problems in setting up a project of this kind."

"What problems?"

"Erm ... Yes, it might actually be too difficult."

"Have you ever seen pictures of tanks hit by so-called depleted uranium bullets?"

Fleischmann answers with a nod of his head.

"Are those effects compatible with the use of so-called depleted uranium?"

"DU weaponry ... that's the dark side of this story. If you look at what happens to the tanks and the people inside them, you can come to some very awkward conclusions ...."

"What do you mean?"

"The energy yield is too great."

"So there must be a different source of energy, then?"

"There's obviously a powerful energy source in so-called depleted uranium weapons ... and yet it's not clear why they use them. In fact, the British Armed Forces are now using titanium ... That old tale that uranium was used because it had a very heavy nucleus was really quite unconvincing. So we're not talking about so-called depleted uranium, it's something else ... I think that a weapon using depleted uranium may not necessarily work in the conventional way."

"Could it use a different technique, such as cold fusion?"

"Who the hell knows?" answers the professor, spreading his arms and smiling. "I hope not, but it's actually possible."

"Why do you think that the explanations given so far about how depleted uranium works cannot be believed?"

"The extremely high temperature reached within the limited space of a tank cannot possibly be explained in terms of the explosion of materials that we currently know about. That's one line. And there's enough information available now to indicate that there are strange products, minor products emanating from the explosions, whose existence can't be explained in those terms ... So, I think it would make sense to envisage a nuclear-type process."

"How could this nuclear process be explained? Can one say fusion? Or fission?"

"I think that the materials observed when using depleted uranium can be explained in terms of fission, depleted uranium fission."

"Why?"

"From observing the materials, they're consistent with the double volcano operation35 which illustrates the products of a fusion reaction."

"You've done research on cold fusion, which is a new nuclear process. Have you noticed any similarity between cold fusion and the effects of depleted uranium?"

"When we studied the cold fusion phenomenon, we obviously analyzed the possible developments of all related processes, which led us to the work of Bridgman in the thirties and forties. Even if some of those studies were misinterpreted, the existing material led us to believe that the fields of depleted uranium weapons and cold fusion might have fallen within a common area. Or, to put it more simply, if we had been able to understand one of the two phenomena, it would have been useful for developing the other one, too."

"Are you referring to determining a general law for all nuclear effects?"

"The true affinity between the two phenomena is the transfer of heat in the systems. If there are nuclear processes, then heat is transferred in the lattice. This transfer takes place in cold fusion, just as it does with so-called depleted uranium weapons."

"Your explanation is that there is a wide-ranging blast effect."

"To explain the incredible transfer of heat in the systems, there must be some long range interaction."

"Do you mean long range in a certain time span?"

"In space and time. Compared to normal processes, it occurs instantaneously. But of course, it is not instantaneous in terms of physics processes in defined spaces. In cold fusion, the transfer of heat can be explained ... it is quite understandable. But if that process is used, or not, in DU weaponry, I can't say. But it'd be interesting to find out."

"If your hypothesis were correct, we'd be faced with a new nuclear process. The consequences suffered by the military and other people in the area might well be caused by nuclear processes, and not by the materials like so-called depleted uranium. Is that possible?"

"Yes. We thought that warfare using depleted uranium weapons raised many questions. And these questions require considerable research before those arms are used."

"Do you think the nuclear process, which is responsible for the heat and production of materials that did not previously exist, may be the cause of the negative effects that depleted uranium has on the people who use it?"

"That's what it looks like. I think that the patchy information we have shows that "strange" elements are produced, which might stem from a fission phenomenon."

"Do you think the military who produce and use such weapons are aware of their nature and the effects that they cause?"

"They use them as weapons. Why should they try to understand anything more than what this job asks of them?"

"But these weapons cause huge damage, even for the people who handle them!"

"Well, that's just the way it goes. If you use weapons whose modus operandi is not fully understood, you'll probably run into phenomena that can't be explained. I definitely think it'd be useful to understand the processes that occur in so-called depleted uranium munitions, and I believe much of this information could be made available if the physical injuries caused by these weapons were properly cataloged. We'd be able to make great strides forward."

"Do you think it's possible to use the potential of nuclear processes differently, in a socially acceptable fashion?"

"I certainly hope so. That was the goal we set ourselves. And there's no reason to believe that we've reached the end of the road in building these devices. I think we should find a way to develop fusion processes, going beyond the existing systems which bombard targets with high energy particles ... we should use some type of cold fusion device."

"Some people say there's a sort of Tutankhamen curse on anyone who touches a certain subject, like cold fusion. Sooner or later, they'll find themselves in big trouble."

"That's a possible interpretation," says the professor, smiling. "One might say that the information available to us supports this conclusion. But whether it's true or false is not the point. There's no way of proving it, without first finding the people responsible for a strategy of that kind."

"Some of the people we interviewed described the state of the bodies left on the ground after the battle at Baghdad airport: the coffins holding the corpses were very small, because the bodies seemed to have shrunk ... they were no longer than a meter. Based on your studies, can you explain this effect? One of the effects of hydrogen-charged uranium is that, beyond a certain limit, energy is released and the hydrogen isotopes expand, combining with oxygen ... so they absorb and eliminate oxygen, and at the same release energy and heat. Might the effect you described be compatible with the shorter bodies found on the battlefield?"

"Yes."

"Is it possible that the negative effects on people caused by the dust were produced by the explosion, rather than the fact that these materials derive from depleted uranium?"

"This point of view should be taken into serious consideration. I think it'd be very unwise, in every stage of such a phenomenon, to rule out any line of research whatsoever, simply because it doesn't match up to some strategy dictated by our existing knowledge. If depleted uranium weapons cause some sort of nuclear interaction, then these interactions must first of all be understood."

"Are you aware of any ongoing project?"

"No. I have no information about any such thing. But I wouldn't be surprised to hear that they're moving in that direction."

During lunch, which takes place in a small restaurant near the cottage, the interview is momentarily interrupted. But Claudio cannot help thinking about what the professor has said. Even though Fleischmann was careful not to make specific accusations, he had not excluded the hypothesis that, by charging uranium with deuterium, a perfect primer for a weapon could be obtained. Neither had the professor confirmed the rumor according to which he himself had carried out a test to charge uranium, an experiment which had apparently caused a huge explosion and "fusion" of the laboratory floor. So it was just a rumor. Quite unconfirmed, in fact.

As far as depleted uranium was concerned, he had been even clearer: that something was not "working in the conventional way" was obvious, but from that to the actual use of some sort of cold fusion technique ...

However, etiquette requires that no one should speak about work during lunch: and in fact, Claudio and Fleischmann find themselves chatting amicably about people they both know and conferences held by a professor at the Italian institute of philosophy in Naples.

Chapter Twenty-One

Confirmation of the Mysterious Telephone Call

Once back at the cottage, the interview begins again, but slowly, with long periods of silence.

"Let's go back to the eighties, when you left the United Kingdom to work in the United States. Tell me about those years ... for five years you all worked in absolute secrecy, didn't you? No one knew what you were doing?"

"No, not officially at least. But there's no way of knowing if the people involved in the project spoke about it to others ... I was convinced that ... as far as I know ... we were working in secret."

"In 1988, you received a call from Washington. Correct?"

"Yes. From 1988 on, we started to make contact with some people at the Department of Energy in Washington DC."

"Was it you who looked for them?"

"Yes."

"So then what happened?"

"Some people came to meet us ... and we talked about our work and its implications."

"What was the official reaction in Washington?"

"I don't know, I think they thought we were all mad," answers the professor, laughing out loud.

"They didn't know what you were talking about ..."

"Exactly."

"I imagine there's one day in your life that you remember in every little detail: March 23, 1989 ..."

"A really bad day. It's hard to remember exactly what happened ... anyway, the University of Utah obviously wanted to be protected by having a patent on our work. I thought it was premature and that we wouldn't be able to get one and that, in fact, is exactly what happened."

"Was the decision to hold a press conference made by the university's governing board?"

"Yes, to get the patent ... and we didn't object."

"Had something happened in the previous days or weeks that convinced you to speed up the process?"

"Yes."

"Please tell me."

"A colleague at Brigham Young University had decided to make that fateful announcement ... which meant we had to communicate the aim of our research to our university. And the university, in turn, decided that we had to be protected by a patent."

"A few days after the conference on March 23, while you were traveling to London, you had to stop in San Francisco. What strange thing happened there?"

"It was the summer of 1989 and I hadn't managed to find a direct flight to London. My only option was to go via San Francisco, but I arrived too late to catch the connecting flight to London. So, I had no choice but to spend the night there ... and I received a telephone call from Edward Teller at the hotel."

"How did he know you were in San Francisco?"

"I haven't the slightest idea, but it shouldn't be difficult to find out."

"Did you tell anyone that you were spending the night there?"

"If you have the power to ask an airline where a passenger is, it's probably not too difficult to find out."

"How did Edward Teller know which hotel you were staying at?"

"That's a good question ... the only thing I can tell you is that he knew where I was."

"Was someone following you?"

"I presume so."

"Did you ever realize you were being followed?"

"No, but since I didn't suspect it, I never noticed a thing."

"Who was Edward Teller?"

"He was the father of the hydrogen bomb."

"What do you remember about him?"

"A striking man and a great physicist."

"Did you meet him in Washington?"

"Yes, afterwards I met him in Washington."

"Can you please tell me about that meeting."

"It was a meeting organized to discuss the work we had done. As far as I remember, we were at the National Science Foundation ..."

"How did he act?"

"Like an interested scientist. He wanted to establish what we had done and I think we managed to explain that to him."

"What was his position at that time?"

"I think he was a consultant at the National Laboratory in Livermore, founded by the Department of Energy."

"He was also a member of the JASON Group ...."

"Was he? That wouldn't surprise me," he said, with a little smile.

"What was the JASON Group?"

"An informal and rather peculiar group of scientists who worked as consultants for the government's scientific policy team. Consultancy that might or might not be taken into consideration."

"Did this group have particular political leanings?"

"No, I don't think so. At that time, it was a think tank headed by Dick Garwin, head of research at Bell Labs."

"Are you aware of any connection between Edward Teller and the military?"

"Given that he had produced the hydrogen bomb ... are there any ties stronger than that? Anyway, he continued to work with them even afterwards."

"Was he merely a consultant or did he have a more structured relationship with them?"

"You can't even imagine how close the ties with certain organizations might be... especially if they're interested in the military applications of nuclear energy."

"Did you ever feel that cold fusion was something that scientists close to the military had already discovered?"

"I often wondered ... if there was anything else brewing ..."

"Did Teller seem surprised by what you had discovered?"

"I had the impression that he was very calm about it ... he absorbed the information he was given, but gave no similar information."

"What did he say when he called you at the hotel room in San Francisco?"

"He asked a series of questions about how to improve the experiment ... they were clearly trying to repeat it. But I really couldn't say if they had already done so."

"Did you get the feeling that someone else already knew what you had discovered?"

"Perhaps ... nothing would surprise me anymore."

"Did Teller subsequently follow the developments in your studies?"

"I presume so."

"But not directly with you, right?"

"I had no further contact with him."

"Did any of you ever think that your lives might be in danger because of the things you had discovered?"

"No, and anyway the steps I took were all dictated by the awareness that it was definitely "advisable" to, as they say, be on my guard ... it was better to be in the limelight of public opinion if I wanted to be safe."

"You and Professor Preparata both suffered from the same illness. Do you think that was a coincidence?"

"It's hard to say, too hard ... It's certainly possible, but... I don't know..."

"Is it true that, according to the Nuclear Energy Act, you risked arrest for your work on cold fusion?"

"I don't know ... but I'll admit to my ignorance," he says, smiling.

"But if you didn't leave the U.S. for that reason, then why did you leave?"

"Because I was disappointed with the line adopted by the university. The best thing I could do was leave."

"But why did you go to France instead of going back to the United Kingdom?"

"Because our sponsors built a laboratory in France. And that was another foolhardy move. But that's what happened."

"So, between 1990 and 1995, you and Stanley Pons worked in southern France for Mr. Toyota.[36] What kind of research were you working on?"

"Cold fusion."

"What kind of agreement did you have with him?"

"We were developing the work."

"Was he interested in producing a certain type of engine that would use cold fusion?"

"Exactly."

"Did it make sense, from a business point of view, that an automobile industry would pay for your research?"

"Yes, it did make sense."

"Some people think that someone built a golden cage around you and Stanley Pons."

"Maybe ... our work moved in a particular direction. If you want to call it a golden cage, that's fine ... but the work we were asked to do was the same as the research done by Preparata and his colleagues in Frascati."

"So they allowed you to study whatever you wanted? They didn't order you to follow a particular line of research ...?"

"We were free to do the research we preferred."

"Were you and Stanley Pons moving in the same direction? In other words, you were not only experimenting with cold fusion as an energy source, but also studying the theoretical bases of this new field. Is that right?"

"We reached an understanding about what was important. But vast resources would have been necessary if we were to proceed in that direction with any success, and we didn't get them."

"After many years of working together, you then followed different paths. What happened?"

"I wish I knew ..." he sighs, pausing for a long moment.

"It had become impossible to continue the work, in that direction at least. The research had been completed and it was not possible to proceed further."

"Did you have different ideas about your future paths?"

"I had my ideas about what was needed, and he undoubtedly had his own views on this subject."

"Did you decide to end your work together for any particular reason?"

"It was all quite contrived ... and here I refer to our disagreements. The issue had become a pretext."

"What do you mean, a pretext?"

"All our differences could have been resolved but ..."

"You mean he'd already decided to follow a different path?"

"I believe so. I think that's the only logical interpretation of those events."

"Did he tell you anything about the path he wished to follow?"

"No."

"Did you form any impression about it?"

"I don't know. I wanted to understand what effect electromagnetic fields might have on the release of energy ... that was the main line of approach to studying deuterium-charged uranium and then studying the effect it might have on energy release. In other words, a research field very similar to the work of Preparata and his group in Frascati."

"Eugene Mallove said that the first review of fusion by MIT was full of prejudiced opinions about you two. Why did MIT and other traditional scientific institutions want to "kill" cold fusion at birth?"

"Because they were very interested in hot fusion. Perhaps that was not the only reason, but it's certainly reason enough to explain their behavior."

"Did MIT and the others fear that cold fusion might divert major public funding from their projects?"

"I think that 1989 was a particularly difficult year ... work on hot fusion had reached a point at which it was necessary to develop a new Tokamak[37] or anyway a new-generation device. It was also the fiftieth anniversary of the discovery of nuclear fission ... so ..."

"It was the year marking the end of the Cold War ..."

"Also. I think that the congressional committee responsible for scientific research was opposed to the idea of starting new large-scale projects."

"What do you think of Eugene Mallove's work?"

"Definitely excellent ... are you talking about the review? Absolutely necessary."

"Did you know that Eugene Mallove was murdered in 2004?"

"No, I didn't know that. It seems very strange ..."

"This story is full of very strange events ...."

"It's always tempting to try and interpret phenomena on the basis of a possible conspiracy theory ... but that should be done only as a last resort, when all other explanations fail. Only then should the possibility of a plot be taken into consideration."

"Let's get back to us. Will devices based on cold fusion ever become commercially available?"

"They will, and the timing depends only on how much money people are prepared to spend. I already have a work program in mind that could very quickly produce a device to be launched on the market."

"Do you think there would be many competing companies or only one monopoly company?"

"I'd say many companies ... and many patents. God knows how many patents have already been registered! But the real question is how many of them will stay on the market. Everything will depend on the skill of their lawyers."

"Cold fusion promises an unlimited source of clean and cheap energy... it's virtually impossible to control in terms of monopoly power. Is this what frightens the establishment?"

"That was said in a somewhat simplistic manner ... but it's certainly an issue. The strangest and most surprising thing about this story is that there was no support for our work ... government support, given that there was the possibility of creating a clean energy source."

"Do you ever dream of being able to heat your home with a cold fusion device?"

"Yes, of course. This might be the first use. But it could also be used in the automotive industry. Did you know that more than 50% of global energy is used at a temperature below 70°C? Cold fusion could cope with this demand."

"How do you think you will be remembered?"

"Well, I don't know ... probably as the "savage of science." Which I am not in the least, mind you. I'm a very conventional scientist. But I think I'll be remembered as a savage."

The interview is over and Fleischmann looks very tired.

Claudio collects his equipment and has a taxi called. Once outside, he cannot fail to notice a phrase etched on one of the stones over the doorway, which effectively sums up the interview that he has just recorded: it is a quote from Saint Austell which reads: "Your life may pass, but make sure that your work is well done."

Claudio finds this second part of the interview quite satisfactory, too, and he puts on his headphones to listen to it again while waiting for his flight to Rome at Heathrow airport. As far as he is concerned, the most crucial point in the whole affair is the confirmation of Teller's phone call, a call that cannot but give rise to the suspicion that cold fusion has played a well-defined role in the history of nuclear weapons. Someone very close to Teller or the military was probably already working in absolute secrecy on charging uranium with deuterium. So even while being very discreet, the professor has presented many hypotheses and opened up various scenarios. Claudio has only one regret, enthralled by the interview, he forgets his raincoat at Heathrow airport, but if Paris is worth a mass, this interview will be worth at least one waterproof jacket!

Chapter Twenty-Two

THE VETERAN FROM 1991 AND THE THIRD NUCLEAR BOMB

Summer 2008.

The plane lands at the airport in Charlotte, North Carolina. Claudio is accompanied by Alex, an Italian friend and colleague, who lives in the United States.

"How long have we been waiting for this interview, eh, Alex?"

"Almost two years. I remember you found the Canadian site where Hank first admitted it and then, after a few months, I was able to contact him and arrange a meeting."

"After that, I rushed to New York only to discover that all the interviews we had set up had been canceled because Hank was afraid."

"You can't complain, we set up another investigation on a different topic in just one afternoon."

"Sure, but I lost almost a year of my life that afternoon ... in this profession, a project can always fall through, but you still have to come back from a trip with some material. Do you know what my trump card was on that occasion? Jey. I think I've already told you about him: the guy we only work with online. I called him and said, "Emergency, Jey! All our appointments have been canceled and we have to change the topic." We'd already done research on a very strange subject and that afternoon, connected via Skype, we managed to fix appointments around the United States in only a few hours, one in Maine, one in Florida and the other two in New York, finding some fantastic pieces to close the program. I could never have done it without him. So is it a sure appointment this time?"

"We'll find out now, I guess."

At the end of the moving walkway, a man dressed in black asks Claudio, "Claudio, is that you?"

"Yes, finally Hank."

After mutual pleasantries, Claudio and Alex get into Hank's car and, after a half hour drive, arrive at his house, a ranch house set among trees where he lives with his wife and daughter. Before beginning the interview, Claudio asks if he can look at the documentation that confirms he took part in Desert Storm in 1991. He wants to check which battalion he fought with and what he did. As well as the documents, Hank also shows him an X-ray plate where Claudio can see the image of the bacterium that was injected into his blood to "make him immune" to anthrax: it was a horrifying filiform bacterium, genetically modified, and made up of two cells.

The U.S. had originally sold the genetically modified anthrax to Saddam, so they knew all about the weapon that he might then have used against American soldiers. Which was why they had tried to activate the immune response in soldiers by injecting the bacteria. With Hank, however, the procedure had not worked, and the bacterium had permanently ruined his health. When he came back to the US, the army's behavior prompted him to collect as much information as possible about what had happened during Desert Storm and make it public. And it is from him that Claudio gets confirmation of the hypotheses made by Kurt Grass and Fleischmann.

Claudio had not given up after the failure of the first trip, two years earlier: a few months later, he insisted on setting up another interview. And this time, before the meeting, they had exchanged questions and answers before the actual interview. Now Hank had agreed to appear on video and for the occasion Claudio had broken his habit of using just one camera, requesting the help of Alex.

"Can you introduce yourself?" begins Claudio.

"My name is Hank, I'm a U.S. Army veteran with ten years of military service behind me."

"When were you in Iraq?"

"I was sent to Saudi Arabia in support of troops involved in the military intervention. I started operations on 25 September 1990 and left Saudi Arabia on February 16, 1991."

"Is there anything that has never been revealed?"

"The U.S. military, together with their allies, dropped a nuclear bomb of about five kilotons – the so-called variable yield nuclear bomb – on the Basra area in Iraq."

"What kind of weapon was it?"

"The weapon is essentially a high-efficiency penetration bomb. When released, it penetrates the objective's interior. In this case, it penetrated the ground and exploded below the surface. It was also used to make certain areas inaccessible. This means that, in practice, the entire area is irradiated. It's also a very effective message if you want to tell someone to stay away from that place. It's called the "Bunker Buster." A five-kiloton nuclear bomb is a relatively small bomb, smaller than the one dropped on Hiroshima, which was sixteen kilotons, or on Nagasaki, which was twenty-two kilotons. The effects of the radioactivity are, however, equally terrible."

"Aren't you afraid to talk about these things?"

"There comes a moment when you have to say 'enough is enough', and when you cross that line there aren't many people who stand beside you. Either you do it, or you don't. When I was in the army, I raised my right hand and vowed 'This I will defend.' But there's a limit to everything."

But who is Hank? This is what Claudio managed to find out about him before the interview: born in 1965, he joined the army at 22, becoming a mechanical engineer in the tenth Mountain Division at Fort Drum. He participated in Desert Storm in Saudi Arabia between September 1990 and February 1991. Returning home because of family problems, he began to suffer from strange disorders. Like other veterans, he began a long battle to have his illness recognized. In 1997 he received an official reprimand after several arguments and was degraded from fourth to third-level engineer. The lower level meant that he could no longer perform his former job and so he was discharged, but with honor. His activity in the veterans' organization of the American army thrust him into the mainstream press – he was quoted in a 2003 article in the *New York Times*, for example – and he was heard by the Presidential Advisory Committee on Gulf War Veterans' Illnesses.

When he came back from Desert Storm, he founded the veterans' organization, Gulf Watch Intelligent Networking System. Hank spoke for the first time about the use of a small nuclear bomb on a Canadian site, using a pseudonym. This is, however, his first television interview on the subject.

"In your opinion, why was it used?"

"From the information I've managed to obtain and verify, the best explanation is that it was used to send a message to Saddam, a message like: 'We are determined to end this war and win the conflict.' The main point is that no matter what the result, it would have been positive for the United States. They could even have dropped this bomb in some more deserted area, and in this way it might have been recognized for what it was, or not recognized, given that it exploded partly underground ... a smaller version of the characteristic mushroom cloud might have appeared. But if it had exploded too far away, no-one would have understood what was happening. The effects had to be perceived immediately and over the long term."

"During Desert Storm, so-called depleted uranium shells were used for the first time. Can you tell me why?"

"So-called 'depleted' and 'non-depleted' uranium both have a kind of radioactive signature. This allows them to be confused with one another. With so-called 'depleted uranium,' the immediate effects caused on individuals, buildings and vehicles also mimic to some extent the effects caused by a bigger nuclear explosion, like the drying out of bodies, the immediate destruction of roads, loss of blood from the eyes and nose. So-called 'depleted uranium' bullets also release small amounts of radiation, but if these bullets are used repeatedly, one projectile immediately after another, as occurs with the machine guns on the A-10 plane, they can cause a strong radioactive impact, both through the dust which is released and the dust given off by the explosion of the projectiles."

"So it was used to cover up...?"

"It could have covered up pretty much everything that happened."

"Are there witnesses?"

"Yes. I was able to talk to some people who were there at that time and I know of others who talked to different people ... I know it sounds strange, but that's how the Intelligence Community works: you get information from one person, you compare it with information from another person and in the end you get the full story. No government in the world will ever admit to having done something like this."

"How did you hear about it?"

"The organization that I created has tried for many years to collect this information in order to make it public and keep it from happening again. Because I can guarantee that if they were able to get away with it in 1991 and 2002, they'll continue to do so as long as they're allowed to, and this has to end."

"These bombs were used at the same time as other warheads: the FAEs, so-called aerosol explosive bombs, also known as MOABs, which produce the same effects as a nuclear bomb, including the mushroom cloud, but without radioactive pollution. Whereas the problem with a nuclear warhead is that when it explodes, it not only detonates, but also releases radioactive pollution."

"Do you think they've been used on other occasions?"

"In Afghanistan, in 2002."

"Can you be more specific about the dates?"

"Yes, between the first and third of March."

Chapter Twenty-Third

VERIFICATION OF THE VETERAN'S ACCOUNT AND THE 'CALCULATED AMBIGUITY' DOCTRINE

It has taken Claudio two years to get this interview, but he is only half way to his goal. Now he has to find confirmation of what the veteran has told him. The information, even if not direct, is quite detailed. One question, in particular, continues to haunt Claudio: how can he possibly check the information? When he returns from his trip, Claudio speaks about it constantly with his colleagues in the newsroom.

"I could look for someone else who knows something and wants to talk about it, maybe one of the witnesses mentioned by Hank. That would be the most obvious solution ... but Hank told me not to do that, and on my own it could take me another two years," says Claudio.

"Try to call some of our sources," suggests Diesel.

"But I can't, it'd be embarrassing ... I can't call one of our sources and ask them, "Listen, I just met a veteran from the first Gulf War who told me they used a 5 kiloton nuclear bomb in Iraq, how do you suggest I verify this information?" They'd think I was crazy.

"Wait, I know – the seismic data ... I could see if, in the period of the first Gulf War, a seismic event with a potency equivalent to five kilotons ever occurred in the area between Basra and the border with Iran. The kilotons can be converted into magnitude on the Richter scale because, during the Cold War, the main activity of the seismic centers was to control nuclear tests in the Soviet Union. So first I have to find a table which compares kilotons to the Richter scale, and then an earthquake with a magnitude of five kilotons in that area. So, Desert Storm lasted 43 days and, if I'm not mistaken, ended on February 28, 1991."

The comparison table between kilotons and the Richter magnitude scale can be found on the Internet. You have to be a bit careful, because it is a logarithmic scale. In practice, magnitude 4 on the Richter Scale is equivalent to 1 kiloton, whereas magnitude 5 is equivalent to 35 kilotons, so a magnitude of 4.1-4.2 corresponds to approximately five kilotons.

Researching the seismological archive is decidedly more complicated: Claudio finds a European archive, the International Seismological Center which, however, has one fault: although formally open to all, it will not give you any data unless you work for a seismological center. Desperately searching for a seismologist or vulcanologist, Claudio leaves his basement office for the newsroom floor, and races around frantically asking everyone, "Sorry to disturb you but does anyone here have a seismologist friend?"

"I've got a psychoanalyst friend ... would he be any good?" answers the first.

"You're too late. There's already been a tsunami," says another, in the same ironic tone.

"Have you upset the director with one of your investigations?" says the last, sarcastically.

Finally, in the culture and entertainment department, his question is answered at last, "Yes, a former high school friend of mine works at the Udine seismic center."

"Numbers of his office and mobile phones, and reliability estimate?" asks Claudio.

"She was one of the best in our class, tell her I gave you her number."

Claudio improvises a painful phone conversation with the seismologist, inventing a friend of his daughter's, who has to do a short thesis for a supplementary exam and needs a list of the seismic events recorded during Desert Storm – a totally unbelievable story. At the end of the call, he is assured that, within a day or two, he will receive a transcript of all the seismic events that occurred in that time frame, within a radius of five hundred miles of Basra.

Only a few minutes after Claudio hangs up, the phone of the editor who had given him the number rings. It is the editor's friend who says Claudio should not worry. She has perfectly understood what he is looking for and will not talk about it to anyone but him.

The next day, the e-mail he is expecting arrives: the data are clear and understandable and above all have been recorded by nine different seismic centers. One of the two events was exactly magnitude 4.2 and it was recorded in the area described by Hank, between the cities of Basra and the border with Iran.

Cataloged under the number 342793, it occurred on February 27 1991, on the last day of the conflict, at precisely 13:39. The phenomenon was recorded by two seismic centers in Iran, four in Nepal, one in Canada, one in Sweden and one in Norway. Its depth was placed at the first surface level ranging from 0 to 33 kilometers.

The figures leave Claudio breathless. The second seismic data, recorded during the period of Desert Storm, record a magnitude of 5.1, corresponding to more than thirty-five kilotons, a nuclear bomb too large to pass unnoticed. The date of this seismic event is February 14, the location several kilometers northwest of Basra and Claudio decides not to take it into consideration.

The first event, however, in the area of Basra, has all the necessary characteristics of the chosen candidate, above all the date: the last day of the war, February 27 1991. The only two nuclear bombs ever used in a conflict were deployed on August 6, 1945 in Hiroshima, and in Nagasaki on August 9, whereas Japan unconditionally surrendered on August 14, 1945.

On February 27, all the forces deployed in Iraq had already returned to Saudi Arabia and there were no U.S. Army units left in the area around Basra.

Encouraged by these facts, Claudio tries to find out if there was a 'smoking gun' element that might have justified a nuclear war scenario of this kind. What event could have convinced the U.S. administration to use a mini-atomic bomb on the last day of the war? Claudio researches the available dateline regarding the first Gulf War and, as he puts the information together, a suspicion begins to take shape: on 25 February, two days before the hypothetical decision to drop an atomic bomb, a Scud missile launched by the Iraqis managed to hit the American base at Dhahran in Saudi Arabia, killing twenty-eight American soldiers and wounding a further ninety-nine. It was a very strange episode because it was the first time a Scud had killed so many people.

In a short article, even the Wall Street Journal pointed out the inconsistencies in the official version of that incident. The incident provoked a harsh reaction by the U.S. army: in the night between 26 and 27 February an entire column of cars and tanks, which were fleeing towards the Kuwaiti border along what has since been named the Highway of Death, was destroyed.

"It may not have been the only act of retaliation ..." says Claudio, thinking out loud. "This is just guesswork ... but U.S. policy in 1991 was deliberately ambiguous. Let's reread the chronology of events in that conflict: August 2, 1990 Saddam Hussein invades Kuwait; 16 January 1991, President Bush announces to the world that Desert Storm has started, the largest military operation since 1948. Twenty-eight countries intervene alongside the U.S. But, at that point, the question was: how would the world of Islam react? That's what most worried the American administration. And also, the U.S. itself had no sure position on the use of a nuclear bomb. Secretary of State, James Baker, stated in this regard: "We want to create the foundations that will put us in the position of having a reasonable cause that justifies the use of (nuclear) force, which is very different from saying that the President has made a decision to move in that direction. We would like this to be a very clear and irrefutable signal, the fact that when the President says he does not wish to exclude the possibility, this means that we believe such an option is credible."

"If Saddam had used chemical or biological weapons, the Pentagon could even have responded with a nuclear weapon.

"But deliberate ambiguity prevailed on the use of nuclear weapons, so much so that Baker himself coined the term 'calculated ambiguity doctrine.' So, in a situation as delicate as that of a conflict in the Middle East, with the risk of causing a generalized uprising in all the countries throughout the area, the U.S. administration, which could no longer rely on the justification of a cold war to use nuclear power, but could not give up on the deterring effect of the threat, either, may have decided to play dirty: use a small tactical bomb and then claim not to have used it, justifying the radiation effects as stemming from depleted uranium. That's exactly what the veteran told me, and he also confirmed that the explosion of depleted uranium bullets had a radioactive effect anyway."

Everything seems to make sense, but it is still not enough. Before broadcasting the interview, Claudio informs the US Department of Defense that an army veteran has revealed the use of a mini-nuclear bomb during Desert Storm. And the Department responds by asking for the date of the alleged use. A very strange answer, as though character A had asked character B if he had ever been to bed with his wife, and B answered, "On what day?" Undoubtedly the Defense Department's answer was consistent with the doctrine of "calculated ambiguity," but it was certainly not reassuring.

Shortly after, Claudius receives the statement from the Pentagon:

> During the 1991 Gulf War, only conventional weapons were used. The United States is in possession of a certain number of weapons with an explosive force of more than 5000 pounds (about two tons), but we cannot confirm the incident you have reported. If a bomb of this potency had been dropped in that area, one could reasonably presume that the detonation would have been recorded by seismic-detection equipment. We repeat again that only conventional weapons were used during the 1991 Gulf War.

In a subsequent letter, the Defense Department informs Claudio that the BLU-82 bomb may have been used, with an explosive force of about seven tons, once again confirming that only conventional weapons had been used. In the light of this statement and the information he has obtained concerning the seismic events, Claudio completes his analysis of the data: a BLU-82 bomb – also called the "mother of all bombs" or "daisycutter" – or other bombs of a similar type (MOAB), first saturate the air with a cloud formed from oxygen, hydrogen and other elements, and then explode with a magnitude of between 2.5 and 3 degrees on the Richter scale and not 4.2 as occurs in the seismic data.[38] This is the bomb which, according to the veteran's account, was detonated at the same time as the nuclear bunker-buster to hide the fact that it was being used.

To be even more certain, Claudio sends an email to the Swedish seismic center that had registered the event and asks if he can have the graph of the recorded waves, thanks to which it will be possible to understand whether it was

an earthquake or an explosion. The seismic center, saying it cannot send the material, adds in its email that "... without a reliable estimate of the depth and relying only on the wave-forms observed by the Swedish stations, the possibility of an explosion cannot be ruled out."

Claudio also films an interview of the eye-witness account given by the former Italian Minister of the Environment, Gianni Mattioli, who had worked ceaselessly at that time to help the people affected by tumors in Basra, and was then decisively blocked by NATO: "I learned that there was a specific objection, an outright prohibition by ... NATO."

It is hard to find doctors who are familiar with the extent of the damage caused by radiation in the area around Basra, and who are also willing to talk about it. Claudio first tries to contact an Iraqi doctor, now living in Syria who, however, after an initial willingness to talk, later refuses to help because she fears for the lives of her loved ones who are still in Iraq. Then, after many problems, he manages to contact the director of the cancer department at the hospital in Basra and arranges a meeting in Istanbul where the doctor is attending a conference.

The interview takes place in his hotel room.

"The history of radiation began during the first Gulf War in 1991," begins Jawad al Ali, "when about three hundred tons of so-called depleted uranium missiles and bombs were dropped on Basra. This led to an increase in the amount of radiation compared to its natural level which, in fact, was very low in Basra. This attack, in 1991, was the most aggressive. They completely destroyed the city's infrastructure ... it was no longer possible to travel from Basra to Baghdad. It happened again in 2003, and this time hundreds of tons of depleted uranium were released in areas inhabited by ordinary people. This caused an increase in tumors and congenital malformations. The question here is simple: it was a clear attempt to exterminate the Iraqi population by poisoning the country's soil and water resources, using poison that will continue to affect future generations."

"Is it difficult to do research on radioactivity in Basra?"

"They don't want anyone to speak about radiation, except for the official spokespeople, and we don't fall into that category. Of course, we can do our research on the spread of cancer, but we cannot do studies on the risk factors ... they don't fund any research of that kind. You can do epidemiological or clinical research but no studies on radiation or anything relating to that sector."

But despite these prohibitions, over the years Ali has collected numerous data, that when collated and compared, permit an initial truth to emerge. "This graph shows a significant increase in the mortality rate caused by tumors in Basra: from the thirty-four cases in 1989, we reached more than six hundred in 2001. I've collected a large number of photographs of the strangest cases, such as malignant fibrous histiocytoma.... These tumors are very rare and closely linked to radioactive pollution.

"And it is the children who are most affected ... the tumors seem to occur in age groups that are different from before. Some types of tumor, which previously appeared in elderly patients, now occur in children only six years old ... this is extremely rare! It's very rare, for example, for a tumor to occur in the lymphatic system of children under ten.

"The other photos relate to some families in which more than one case of cancer has occurred in the same nucleus. I've studied about thirty-one cases of this kind, with more than one relative affected by cancer ... and the number of families has increased to seventy-one. In these cases, too, we are talking about very rare occurrences."

The disastrous effects of the war in Basra are evident. Claudio talks to Dr. Ali about the hypothesis that, in addition to tons of dirty uranium, a mini-bomb may also have been used. But the doctor appears skeptical about this, because he thinks that something of that kind could not have gone unnoticed.

Nonetheless, he shows Claudio photos of some children who died in his hospital, as though they were cards in a macabre game that it is almost impossible to figure out: "This is Isra: she was fifteen years old, suffered from acute leukemia and died; this is Wala: she was five and had an ovarian tumor, very rare at that age, since it's usually a pathology affecting middle-aged women; this boy, who was only five years old, had non-Hodgkin's lymphoma which is very rare under the age of ten, and died on the day he arrived at the hospital; this girl is Sheda, she was twelve and had bone cancer that spread ... her arm was amputated, but it served no purpose and she also died; this boy had a very large head, full of liquid, and similar photos were taken in Hiroshima after the explosion of the atomic bomb ..."

The doctor continues with his sad list of these little angels as though he were reciting a rosary. Children killed by a disease they did not understand, caused by reasons of which they were totally unaware. The only thing that we now know is that the first person to suggest the military use of this radioactive and invisible dust, capable of annihilating enemy populations, was the rector of a major American university.

Chapter Twenty-Four

Mysterious Weapons
in Gaza

O n the Internet, Claudio manages to intercept the alarm sounded by several doctors in Gaza: they report inexplicable wounds which have led to the amputation of a lower limb in at least eighty cases. Doctors have repeatedly asked the international community for help in understanding the causes of these strange wounds, in which there are small fragments, often invisible in X-rays, as well as incomprehensible amputations of the lower limbs caused by what appears to be an extremely strong blast of heat. But no one has responded to their appeal.

Through Skype, Claudio manages to make contact with some Palestinian doctors and gather information on the effects of these devices. In the course of his conversations, he succeeds in identifying the emblematic case of a medical worker who was injured in a small street far away from the areas that were usually affected by the fighting. So he decides to leave for Gaza to collect further information.

Crossing the border through the Erez terminal between Israel and Gaza is a sort of humiliating rite of passage to which a journalist must submit when going over to the other side. Interminable and deliberately useless periods of waiting, created with the sole aim of discouraging the foreign media; a meticulous analysis of the reasons for the journey and of one's credentials, all strictly above-board of course, but unbearably slow. Then that caged passage, several hundred meters long, through no man's land, which takes the traveler into the largest prison in the world. This time Claudio is expected and the situation is less complicated; the only thing requested of him is to carefully calculate his movements, the places he will be visiting, and his carers, so as to reduce the risk of something happening to him. The work begins by interviewing a cameraman from the local television station.

"I was filming in the Al Aqsa Martyrs' hospital ... it was dawn and they had brought the first three wounded people, one of whom was in fact the ambulance driver, Abdul. I noticed that all the wounded had amputated legs ... those who arrived later also had similar amputations and I asked myself what kind of weapons the Israelis were using. I noticed that the injuries were never more than one meter and ten centimeters above ground."

Next comes a doctor from Al Shifa hospital: "In the final raid by the Israelis, we doctors noticed that all the wounded had strange injuries and severe burns ... in many cases, the bullet fragments could not be seen from the outside. The amputated limbs were always legs ... sometimes one, sometimes both ... and the smaller blood vessels were already partially closed off, whereas the larger ones continued to bleed. The area around the amputation was black, burnt ... necrosis of the tissues had already set in, they were hardened, and the injury seemed old even if it had only happened a few minutes before ... the wounds were terribly infected, the limb had been completely severed, as if a saw had been used to cut through the bone and all the tissues. We managed to identify some non-metallic fragments in the tissue. From our analyses, we realized that they were optically radio invisible, which means that X-rays pass through them but don't detect them."

The case of an ambulance driver was emblematic: "I was going back to my colleague to help more wounded people, when suddenly a rocket launched by a remote controlled airplane fell out of the sky ... we were in the open and we didn't see any soldiers at the windows or tanks in the area ... the explosion of the bomb sounded very close, I fell down and when I tried to stand up, I saw a TV camera man filming me. Then they took me away with some other guys ... and I looked at my leg which had been cut off at almost knee-level. I didn't hear any noise, only a screech, a whistle ... there are electronic materials among the fragments, similar to the ones in a radio or television, so that's why I think they're electronic weapons launched by aircraft ... they can't be seen until they hit the target."

Later Claudio goes to the area where this event took place and notices that there is much less damage to the surrounding environment than to the people. But what kind of weapon was used in Gaza? It appears to have two main features: the fragments that are invisible to X-rays, and the strong blast of heat that can even cut through bones. But to find an explanation to this mystery, Claudio needs help from his colleagues, so he decides to mobilize all the forces at his disposal: the two assistants, the journalists in the newsroom and even Jey, locked away in his retreat. Everyone contributes to the research in an attempt to trace a weapon whose effects are compatible with those seen in Gaza.

They systematically analyze all the sites dealing with military technology, and at last find something: on the site of the magazine, *Defense Tech*, there is a description of a new remote-controlled weapon fired from unmanned drones that can minimize environmental damage. It is a small diameter bomb consisting of a carbon fiber casing which, when it explodes, shatters into micro-shrapnel. The bombs are packed with tungsten powder, aimed at the target using a particular angle, and as they become charged with energy, accurately destroy everything in their path within a range of four meters. The bomb is known as DIME (Dense Inert Metal Explosive). As well as describing the bomb, the article warns of the possible carcinogenic effects of tungsten.

Claudio decides to go back to the doctor at Al Shifa hospital to see if this weapon might actually be the one used.

"Yes, it might be compatible with the one used by Israel. It spreads a kind of dust that burns the entire surface of the body ... We found small invisible wounds, dust inside and outside of tissues, and even fragmentation of the liver and spleen without there having been any rupture of the tissues."

Then, taking advantage of the compulsory journey back through Israel and tired of the formal responses coming from the Ministry of Defense: "Israel does not use weapons that are prohibited by international law" – Claudio decides to turn to the country's foremost expert in weapons.

The former general he interviews, gives him further elements: "This new type of warfare takes place in areas where combatants are mixed with the civilians ... you have to strike with precision without causing too much damage. The bomb you mentioned works in this way, but one cannot always distinguish between terrorists and civilians. If the warhead is small, however, it can only hit one person, like on television when a policeman shoots the terrorist between the eyes as he's hiding behind a hostage. If we can do this from a distance of hundreds of miles, it could make the difference."

Claudio manages to get hold of a fragment from the device, and when he returns to Italy, takes it to be analyzed by a chemistry professor who is always willing to offer suggestions and ask questions, and enthusiastically follows all his "investigative" broadcasts. The results of the analyses reveal that the main element is carbon, but there are also compounds of metallic elements such as tungsten and silica.

Due to the technology that DIME weapons use, they come under the new category of "low lethality" weapons, i.e., weapons that are able to "minimize" collateral damage and restrict their lethal effects to a limited area. The devices can have various sizes and functions, but the one described in *Defense Tech* uses tungsten powder, a heavy metal used in many hydrogen *loading* experiments in order to produce so-called cold fusion. The hypothesis that *the kind of "energetic" loading of tungsten* is in fact the same thing as charging tungsten with hydrogen, seems to be entirely plausible. A hypothesis that is also reinforced by the fact that the wounds self-cauterize shortly after the explosion, and that the organic material does not seem to respond to traditional treatment. These effects may be compatible with the release of hydrogen atoms, which tend to bind with oxygen, literally sucking it out of the organic matter with which they come into contact.

Hoping to understand things better, Claudio seeks solace on the phone from Kurt Grass who, as usual, is ready to lend a hand.

"Let's assume that this tungsten powder contains an extremely high percentage of hydrogen and that, on impact, external pressure or an internal explosion caused it to reach the threshold of the Bridgman effect, with the subsequent production of nanoparticles. So at the moment of impact, hydrogen would be released in atomic rather than molecular form. At this stage, the hydrogen would be exceptionally active from a chemical standpoint, and would thus have an extraordinary affinity with the oxygen contained in the human targets' biological material, "stealing" its oxygen and causing the bodies to collapse by chemical means. An eventual jet of atomic hydrogen, combining with the oxygen, would create water, which would then pass unnoticed.

And so here is an example of a dynamic act of destruction produced by an extremely intense reaction, because oxygen and hydrogen are two of the strongest chemical reagents. If we then consider that tungsten powder can be packed into carbon micro-tubes which are four hundred times sturdier than steel and much lighter, the accurately aimed explosive force may produce effects very similar to those you have encountered. To cope with this sort of damage to the organism and combat tissue necrosis, the body would have to be re-oxygenated through strongly alkaline aqueous solutions, such as sodium or potassium bicarbonate or, in the most serious cases, cesium chloride. I'm referring to the studies of my friend Vladimir Voeikov, professor of Biorganic Chemistry at Moscow University."[39]

Chapter Twenty-Five

COLD FUSION IS HOT AGAIN

It is a well-known fact that moments of crisis force the world to renew itself. For rich countries, this possibility of innovation can be seen in clean technologies, which become a sector that induces global economic recovery. And among the clean technologies, so-called "cold fusion" cannot be ignored.

60 Minutes, the investigative program on CBS, the network that was viewed in the past as the "gold standard" of American news broadcasting, is the first to speak about cold fusion once more.

Its former campaigns against McCarthyism, conducted by Edward R. Murrow, had once been a milestone in the history of journalism. Even though CBS does not enjoy such perfect health today, there are still some excellent journalists and it was towards the middle of 2009 that this TV network broadcast an episode of its investigative program entitled "Cold Fusion Is Hot Again."

Claudio's editorial team downloads the program from the Internet and organizes a group viewing, turning the office into a small film club. Here is a brief excerpt from the transmission: "It promised to be cheap, limitless and clean. Cold fusion would end our dependence on the Middle East and stop those greenhouse gases blamed for global warming. It would change everything. But then, just as quickly as it was announced, it was discredited. So thoroughly, that cold fusion became a catch phrase for junk science. Well, a funny thing happened on the way to oblivion – for many scientists today, cold fusion is hot again."

The program develops in the classic way: an advocate of the validity of cold fusion and a detractor are set face to face. The detractor is then taken to Israel to observe the results and change his mind. Then the inventor of cold fusion, Martin Fleischmann, is interviewed.

The supporter of cold fusion is the electro-chemist, Michael McKubre, who speaks about the fifty experiments he has conducted at SRI International, a respected California lab that does extensive work for the government, and is convinced of the possible positive developments of this invention. More from the transmission on *60 Minutes*: "The potential is for an energy source that would run your car for three, four years, for example. And you'd take it in for service every four years and they'd give you a new power supply."

During the program, there is even time for a demonstration of the scientific experiment, with the aim of showing its relative simplicity. The main "ingredients" are palladium and deuterium, the latter being essentially unlimited. "There is ten times as much energy in a gallon of sea water, from the deuterium contained within it, than there is in a gallon of gasoline." Palladium is placed in water containing deuterium and the third ingredient is an electric current.

The explanation of the physics process is simple to understand in broad terms. At the atomic level, palladium looks like a lattice and the electricity conducts the deuterium to the palladium. "They sit on the surface and they pop inside the lattice," he explains, using an artist's rendering of the lattice. McKubre believes there is a nuclear reaction – possibly a fusion process like what happens in the sun – but occurring inside the metal, at a slower rate, and without dangerous radiation. Scientists today like to call it a nuclear effect rather than cold fusion. At least twenty labs working independently have published reports of excess heat – up to twenty-five times greater than the electricity going in.

According to the researcher McKubre, ".. if there's a one percent chance that Fleischmann and Pons were correct, I now believe that possibility is ninety-nine percent."

60 Minutes then notes that the careers of Fleischmann and Pons were destroyed as quickly as a nuclear flash – names once linked to a Nobel Prize were forgotten by nearly everyone. "And most of the scientific world today is happy to leave things as they are."

Richard Garwin then recalls his participation in the "unfortunate" success of one of the most successful hot fusion experiments in the world: that of the hydrogen bomb. The scientist – already a fierce opponent of cold fusion back in 1989 – thinks that the amount of electricity going in and the heat coming out are simply mis-measured. In addition, he reveals that "the experiments produce excess heat at best seventy percent of the time; it can take days or weeks for the excess heat to show up. And it's never the same amount of energy twice."

McKubre argues that this probably has "something to do with how the palladium is prepared. I'm working with an Italian government lab called ENEA where some of the most reliable palladium is made."

Then *60 Minutes* turns to an independent scientist, Rob Duncan, vice chancellor of research at the University of Missouri and an expert in measuring energy who went to Israel with the program's journalists, where a lab called Energetics Technologies had reported some of the biggest energy gains to date. Duncan spent two days examining cold fusion experiments and investigating whether the measurements were accurate, and finally admitted, "Wow, they've done something really interesting here." He crunched the numbers himself and searched for an explanation other than a nuclear effect. "I found that the work was carefully done, and that the excess heat, as I see it now, is quite real … I never thought I'd say that."

Finally, there is still room for a last scientist, "a man who left America in disgrace and retired with his wife to the English countryside. Martin Fleischmann, the man who announced cold fusion to the world, is hindered by years, diabetes, Parkinson's disease and maybe a little bitterness."

"I have two regrets," begins Fleischmann. "Calling the nuclear effect 'fusion,' a name coined by a competitor, and having participated in that news conference," something he says the University of Utah wanted.

"Now that you know that your experiments have been replicated and improved upon in labs all over the world, I wonder, do you see a day when homes will be powered by these cells, when cars will be powered by these cells?" asks the interviewer.

"I think so. It wouldn't take very long to implement this," Fleischman replies, laughing. "The potential is exciting."

Following the screening, his colleagues look at Claudio in horror. "Surely you don't think that was a good investigation?" asks Diesel.

"I think it's important that the American public rediscovers cold fusion. In fact, I think it's really courageous of CBS to speak so positively about it," replies Claudio.

"But it only says what everybody already knows, that it works and that it still can't quite be controlled," says Sci.

"It says nothing about the reasons why it was canceled from the history of American science ... they meet Fleischmann and don't ask him anything about what the real reasons may have been for the problems he came up against? They don't ask him why he went to work in France with the Japanese, or about his talks with the Department of Energy, and what their position was ..." adds Amba.

"I hear what you're saying: they give the facts but don't explain the reasons. Could *you* explain the reasons?" asks Claudio.

"Well, if nothing else, I'd try, all the analysis of how atomic strategy was modified and nuclear devices miniaturized could help us understand why it was necessary to eliminate critical mass," responds Amba.

"So you're also convinced that the secret hidden away for twenty years is that if uranium is charged with deuterium beyond a critical threshold, it causes a sort of explosion that triggers a fusion-fission process?" asks Claudio.

"We can't be sure how the process works," interrupts Cass, "No one can .. but I think I've understood that it has a radioactive effect, anyway, for example gamma rays, but very limited both in terms of its nuclear mass, and the processes it triggers."

"It doesn't take much imagination to understand it, if you do research on fourth-generation explosive devices," asserts Sci. "Let me refresh your memory: the first generation is the fission model of the Hiroshima nuclear bomb, the second is the hydrogen bomb, the third, the neutron bomb, and the fourth, the miniaturized bomb. Research has shown that some devices hypothesize uranium shielding around the explosive core, according to the level of radioactive pollution that must be produced, because that's no longer a secondary effect imposed by the critical mass of uranium, but a deliberately chosen primary effect. In other words, these small new bombs may have a relatively limited radioactive and pollutant effect, perhaps too limited ... so they're weighted down with outer layers of uranium that increase both the pollutant and explosive effect."

"Guys, as poor students who have just completed a refresher course, you've become very self-confident and articulate, but let me see this research anyway," concludes Claudio. Then, glancing at his colleagues' notes, "We're missing some steps that we can check with Kurt Grass, and then we could also write the history of this twenty-year secret ... but who do you tell about a secret that's lasted that long? Secrets have a life span, just like lies and gossip. Who in today's news world is interested in such an old and terribly complicated conspiracy?"

"Or you could tell the whole thing as if it were a novel, making hypotheses which readers could believe or not

... paraphrasing James Baker, we could create a novel of 'calculated ambiguity,'" proposes Amba.

Suddenly Professor Grass appears at the door. Invited to watch the CBS program, he is decidedly behind time.

"Sorry I'm late, but I haven't come to see the program on cold fusion, which I don't mind missing actually, but because the things I need to talk about couldn't be discussed over the phone."

"Have you discovered something interesting, Professor Grass?" asks Claudio.

"No, nothing ... you guys certainly have a strange idea about truth, as if it were something that already existed, a kind of treasure buried by pirates on a desert island. The truth doesn't already exist, you just have to put it back together again, starting from the pieces into which it has shattered in the real world."

"That's just the point: we journalists can discover the truth, but we can't invent anything."

"Do you remember Lacan's riddle?[40] The one about the five discs ... three white and two black, three of which were fastened between the shoulders of three prisoners, and the one who guessed what color his disc was by looking at the other prisoners' discs, would go to the door, tell the prison warden and go free ... do you remember?"

"Sure."

"If you try to solve it in an abstract way, this riddle has no solution. In fact, if the prison warden fastened three white discs between their shoulders, each of the prisoners would always see two white discs on the other prisoners' backs and have no idea if his disc was black or white. But if you manage to get away from the approach of nineteenth-century physics, in which time is not considered to be a variable, and you think about living in a century adapted to quantum physics, where time is also a variable, then you realize that there is a solution."

"Which is?"

"It's the movement towards the door – even just the possibility or lack of it – which provides the time variable that can solve the riddle. The other mistake is to assume that everyone is stupid, that nobody thinks or is able to make hypotheses. But the three prisoners do in fact think. When Prisoner A sees two white discs on the backs of the other two, he reasons as follows: if I had a black disc, what would happen? B would see a white and a black disk and so he could not make a decision. But B is not stupid and he would think, like A, "If the disc on my back was black, what would happen?" At that point, if B thought he had a black disc and A had a black disk, C would go to the door, stating with certainty that his disk was white. But C doesn't move and so the disc on A's back must be white. So, even though nothing actually happens, it is the time span, together with the hypothetical thought process, which makes it possible to solve the problem.

"You see, Claudio, even if we study a lot, all the books in the world, we do not know and will never know anything, but we can make hypotheses – in fact we can only make hypotheses, and then act accordingly. We can recount these hypotheses well or not so well, but they're still only guesswork.... But if, for different reasons, other people make the same hypotheses, we then start to have a minimum of certainty, and even if nothing happens, things change: they change precisely because, given that nothing happens, you realize that nobody has any certainties and that the only certainty is that faint hypothesis, surrounded by doubt, that we have created.

"So, I too agree that things must be recounted for what they are, i.e. hypotheses. What do you think theoretical physics consists of, if not fragile threads of reasoning – not strings, note well, which are a different story altogether (even though also very hypothetical) – and if you need to make hypotheses, I'll accept that. So let's start to make hypotheses again, let's write our 'novel' whose title could be

137

"The Secret of the Three Bullets." This lends itself perfectly to a three-fold interpretation:

> 1) the official interpretation or rather the first deception: the bullets contain so-called depleted uranium, bullets that may be found in a museum, but are not often used on the battlefield;
>
> 2) the second interpretation, the second deception: bullets made with waste from nuclear reactors (41) and passed off as depleted uranium bullets, actually serve to pollute an area and damage the life forms existing there. The material used is more radioactive than so-called depleted uranium, and there might also be other elements in the mixture, which come into the third interpretation. A 4000°C temperature is not produced by the pyrophoric effect of uranium alone. In his interview, Martin Fleischmann was very clear on this point;
>
> 3) the third interpretation: a nuclear bomb, the size of a bullet, the one responsible for the Khiam crater, produced with deuterium-charged uranium that triggered first fusion and then fission.

I'm not inventing anything ... you have the evidence that the three-card game was done with three different bullets: the official depleted uranium ones that exist almost exclusively in books; the dirty uranium ones with traces of materials produced by fission – that may have occurred in a nuclear reactor or at the moment they exploded, and that anyway serve to increase radioactivity, which will poison the area where they're used and cover up the third type of bullet – the uranium one charged with deuterium, which acts as a primer for a nuclear bomb the size of a bullet. It all makes sense: what Fleischmann said in his interview about how his experiments developed by substituting palladium with uranium to study its potential for fusion and fission; what the Desert Storm veteran said also makes sense, i.e. the use of depleted uranium for the first time in 1991, which made it easier to hide the third type of bullet, the uranium one charged with deuterium, the trigger for a nuclear bomb the size of a bullet. In the specific case of the 1991 bomb, it was perhaps larger than a bullet, because five kilotons would have required two hundred fifty kilograms of natural uranium, a quantity that could have been reduced by using enriched uranium.

"Imagine a con man who plays the three-card game, dropping the cards quickly and asking you several times where the king is ... and you think you've got it, because he always turns up the king where you think it is. Then he quickly swaps the king for the queen, and asks you to bet and you do, convinced that you know where the king is ... but you lose, and the game starts again and you no longer know which card is the king and which the queen, and he tells you to bet again ... and you think you've followed the queen and you pick up the card, and it's the ace instead.

"That's what happens when they drop a bomb that you think is still depleted uranium ... then you do the analyses and discover that it's dirty uranium with fission products. But someone argues that the analyses are not reliable and that traces from previous events are left in the sample ... and in this way, it all seems to make sense and everyone is led to believe that there are huge deposits of natural uranium in Lebanon. Then they drop the real bomb, the nuclear one which creates evident radiation, and for even greater peace of mind, they even eliminate the United Nations observers. Well, this game of the three bullets is now happening in several countries. And even when they scrape the ground they consider too radioactive – declaring that it's been polluted by depleted uranium – and bring the radioactive sand back home ... but what radioactive sand? Wasn't it all supposed to be depleted uranium?[42] And so now, with ambiguity calculated to perfection, the true prohibition is broken, the one that humanity decided nobody could break: the return of nuclear weapons.

"And so the sham goes on: the indignation about the Korean testing, the sanctions against Iran ... all perfectly normal, because no one seems to notice anything.

"Three almost identical devices or bullets: one with depleted uranium, one with slightly enriched uranium that produces fission material, and one with deuterium-charged uranium that can trigger a small nuclear explosion. They look identical: the first destined for the museum, the second for the battlefields, and the third ... Well, the third, the deuterium-charged uranium one, is a true nuclear bomb the size of a bullet, and it was used in Khiam against the underground shelters. Starting with the data collected in Kosovo, Iraq and Lebanon, this is the most concrete interpretation of all those made until now.

"But don't stop there ... we're talking about a new class of weapons that exploits the hydrogen or deuterium charging of heavy metals. So when you see severed legs in Gaza and read that it's a bomb with dense inert and explosive material, remember the rule about adjectives in military acronyms: they mean the opposite. And so, not inert tungsten powder, but deuterium or hydrogen charged powder, and not of generic energy ... even in this case, our hypothesis is more effective than others in explaining the effects ... but we're only at the beginning and we'll see more of these things ... and they won't be pleasant."

"Okay, let's work on it, but without ideological certainties! When I hear the phrase "They've done this ... or that," I get nervous ... they who? We need to identify "Who, how, when and why," so let's get back to work. If everything you've told us is true, and I've no reason to doubt it, we should be able to find the acronyms of the weapons used, the patents of the factories that produced them and the damage caused to workers and the population in the areas of *DejaVu Sans*, like those already reported at the Concord plant, in Massachusetts, and at Starmet Corporation."[43]

"As usual, you're always one step behind, Claudio," interrupts Diesel. "I was checking the mail and found an email from Dr. Garbati. Intrigued by our hypotheses, she started to search for information on patents for new weapons and listen to this:

My dears,

On the Internet, I found a document listing the patents regarding manufacture of new generation weaponry. Reading it carefully – not without a growing sense of unease – the following list of materials emerged: titanium, zirconium, hafnium – which have exactly the same outer electron structure – and then thorium and uranium. These materials have been under study for some time as hydrogen absorbers and are also quite expensive. The idea of using micro- or nano-structured materials stems from the high surface to volume ratio that they have, which is extremely useful for all the chemical processes that take place on the surface. But the thing I found most disconcerting was a patent dating back to 2005.

The deposited text reads as follows: "Background information on the invention: the composite and reactive materials function with particular effectiveness when they are used for the construction of projectiles to destroy protected targets. These protected targets may be objectives defended by a facility construction or an armored structure. At the time when the protected target is struck, the energy released at the moment of impact serves as a catalyst which triggers a chemical reaction of composite materials and reagents. This reaction releases a large amount of energy."

The core of the weapon is a reaction, which is improperly defined as "chemical," and is unleashed upon impact. And then: "As is well-known in this field of science, composite materials and reagents generally include particles or powdered forms of one or more reactive metals. The reactive metals may include aluminum, beryllium, hafnium, lithium, magnesium, thorium, titanium, uranium, zirconium, as well as combinations, alloys and hydrides of these metals."

Note well! Here the word 'hydrides', metal-hydrogen compounds appears. This term is never mentioned again, but the periphrasis 'reactive composite materials' is used instead.

The purpose of this patent is to provide a method for increasing the performance capabilities of the reactive projectile, increasing its release of energy on the target. This is done by adding a 'containment' system to the reactive material, through strips of inert material, which increase its compression. This is one of the key points in the patent.

Another key point is the presence of an elongated structure composed of high density material: "Each of the containers described above will operate in essentially the same way upon impact with the target. That is to say, upon impact, the total additional density provided by the elongated structure increases penetration below the target's surface. So when the elongated structure begins to insert itself, buckling and/or breaking up, this folding up of the material will cause breakage and pulverization of the material inside it. This twisting and pressure serve as a source and trigger for a very strong reaction."

The impact activates the reactive material, placing it in contact with the air or releasing the trapped hydrogen. The elongated central structure is struck by the energy that has developed and receives a high compression wave, producing a further gain in energy. Note that the terms used are break up and shear deformation ... doesn't it bring to mind precisely the Bridgman effect that Professor Grass told us about and that has been excluded from academic debate and specialized magazines for so long?

Reading the patent's text I thought that I had already seen everything, but in another form. It was a patent put out by the Japanese Yoshiaki Arata (Pub. Date: 2005-07-06) in which a method of producing (nuclear) energy is described by confining hydrogen and isotopes (deuterium) in nano-structured form within an inert matrix (zirconium). Here too, the trigger stems from compression waves.

Arata is a very old (he is almost ninety) Japanese physicist, who is very well known and respected in his country. He now operates in the cold fusion sector after decades of study in the thermonuclear fusion field.

I can tell you quite frankly that these issues make me extremely uncomfortable, I can not understand how the extraordinary privilege of having had access to so many secrets concerning matter and the laws which everything obeys, can be used to ... kill. I find it infinitely more repugnant than the war waged with stones and knives by those who have not had the fortune of belonging to our superior Western civilization.

From now on, I would like to stay away from anything that has to do with this issue, even if it means giving up everything I have worked for so far.

Reality is complex and elusive, but responsibility is always individual, don't you think?

Best wishes,

Livia Garbati

"It's a really beautiful letter," says Claudio. "And if we want to lend Dr. Garbati a hand, I think the moment has come to release this story. So let's start working ... we've already got quite enough input. After all, we're not just playing with dolls here!"

Appendix One

LETTER ON THE OPPENHEIMER AFFAIR

From: K.D. Nichols
To: J R Oppenheimer
Date: December 23, 1953

Section 10 of the Atomic Energy Act of 1946 places upon the Atomic Energy Commission the responsibility for assuring that individuals are employed by the Commission only when such employment will not endanger the common defense and security. In addition, Executive Order 10450 of April 27, 1953, requires the suspension of employment of any individual where there exists information indicating that his employment may not be clearly consistent with the interests of the national security.

As a result of additional investigation as to your character, associations, and loyalty, and review of your personnel security file in the light of the requirements of the Atomic Energy Act and the requirements of Executive Order 10450, there has developed considerable question whether your continued employment on Atomic Energy Commission work will endanger the common defense and security and whether such continued employment is clearly consistent with the interests of the national security. This letter is to advise you of the steps which you may take to assist in the resolution of this question.

The substance of the information which raises the question concerning your eligibility for employment on Atomic Energy Commission work is as follows:

It was reported that in 1940 you were listed as a sponsor of the Friends of the Chinese People, an organization which was characterized in 1944 by the House Committee on UnAmerican Activities as a Communist-front organization. It was further reported that in 1940 your name was included on a letterhead of the American Committee for Democratic and Intellectual Freedom as a member of its national executive committee. The American Committee for Democracy and Intellectual Freedom was characterized in 1942 by the House Committee on UnAmerican Activities as a Communist front which defended Communist teachers, and in 1943 it was characterized as subversive and unAmerican by a special subcommittee of the House Committee on Appropriations. It was further reported that in 1938 you were a member of the Western Council of the Consumers Union. The Consumers Union was cited in 1944 by the House Committee on UnAmerican Activities as a Communist-front headed by the Communist Arthur Kallet. It was further reported that you stated in 1943 that you were not a Communist, but had probably belonged to every Communist front organization on the west coast and had signed many petitions in which Communists were interested.

It was reported that in 1943 and previously you were intimately associated with Dr. Jean Tatlock, a member of the Communist Party in San Francisco, and that Dr. Tatlock was partially responsible for your association with Communist-front groups.

It was reported that your wife, Katherine Puening Oppenheimer, was formerly the wife of Joseph Dallet, a member of the Communist Party, who was killed in Spain in 1937 fighting for the Spanish Republican Army. It was further reported that during the period of her association with Joseph Dallet, your wife became a member of the Communist Party. The Communist Party has been designated by the Attorney General as a subversive organization which seeks to alter the form of Government of the United States by unconstitutional means, within the purview of Executive Order 9835 and Executive Order 10450....

It was reported that you have associated with members and officials of the Communist Party including Isaac Folkoff, Steve Nelson, Rudy Lambert, Kenneth May, Jack Manley, and Thomas Addis.

It was reported that you were a subscriber to the *Daily People's World*, a west coast Communist newspaper, in 1941 and 1942....

It was reported that prior to March 1, 1943, possibly 3 months prior, Peter Ivanov, secretary of the Soviet consulate, San Francisco, approached George Charles Eltenton for the purpose of obtaining information regarding work being done at the Radiation Laboratory for the use of Soviet scientists; that George Charles Eltenton subsequently requested Haakon Chevalier to approach you concerning this matter; that Haakon Chevalier thereupon approached you, either directly or through your brother, Frank Friedman Oppenheimer, in connection with this matter; and that Haakon Chevalier finally advised George Charles Eltenton that there was no chance whatsoever of obtaining the information. It was further reported that you did not report this episode to the appropriate authorities until several months after its occurrence; that when you initially discussed this matter with the appropriate authorities on August 26, 1943, you did not identify yourself as the person who had been approached, and you refused to identify Haakon Chevalier as the individual who made the approach on behalf of George Charles Eltenton; and that it was not until several months later, when you were ordered by a superior to do so, that you so identified Haakon Chevalier. It was further reported that upon your return to Berkeley following your separation from the Los Alamos project, you were visited by the Chevaliers on several occasions; and that your wife was in contact with Haakon and Barbara Chevalier in 1946 and 1947.

It was reported that in 1945 you expressed the view that "there is a reasonable possibility that it (the hydrogen bomb) can be made," but that the feasibility of the hydrogen bomb did not appear, on theoretical grounds, as certain as the fission bomb appeared certain, on theoretical grounds, when the Los Alamos Laboratory was started; and that in the autumn of 1949 the General Advisory Committee expressed the view that "an imaginative and concerted attack on the problem has a better than even chance of producing the weapon within 5 years." It was further reported that in the autumn of 1949 and subsequently, you strongly opposed the development of the hydrogen bomb; (1) on moral grounds, (2) by claiming that it was not feasible, (3) by claiming that there were insufficient facilities and scientific personnel to carry on the development and (4) that it was not politically desirable. It was further reported that even after it was determined, as a matter of national policy, to proceed with development of a hydrogen bomb, you continued to oppose the project and declined to cooperate fully in the project. It was further reported that you departed from your proper role as an adviser to the Commission by causing the distribution separately and in private, to top personnel at Los Alamos of the majority and minority reports of the General Advisory Committee on development of the hydrogen bomb for the purpose of trying to turn such top personnel against the development of the hydrogen bomb. It was further reported that you were instrumental in persuading other outstanding scientists not to work on the hydrogen-bomb project, and that the opposition to the hydrogen bomb, of which you are the most experienced, most powerful, and most effective member, has definitely slowed down its development.

In view of your access to highly sensitive classified information, and in view of these allegations which, until disproved, raise questions as to your veracity, conduct and even your loyalty, the Commission has no other recourse, in discharge of its obligations to protect the common defense and security, but to suspend your clearance until the matter has been resolved. Accordingly, your employment on Atomic Energy Commission work and your eligibility for access to restricted data are hereby suspended, effective immediately, pending final determination of this matter.

To assist in the resolution of this matter, you have the privilege of appearing before an Atomic Energy Commission personnel security board. To avail yourself of the privileges afforded you under the Atomic Energy Commission hearing procedures, you must, within 30 days following receipt of this letter, submit to me, in writing, your reply to the information outlined above and request the opportunity of appearing before the personnel security board. Should you signify your desire to appear before the board, you will be notified of the composition of the board and may challenge any member of it for cause. Such challenge should be submitted within 72 hours of the receipt of notice of composition of the board ...

If a written response is not received from you within 30 days it will be assumed that you do not wish to submit any explanation for further consideration. In that event, or should you not advise me in writing of your desire to appear before the personnel security board, a determination in your case will be made by me on the basis of the existing record ...

Very truly yours,
K. D. Nichols,
General Manager

Appendix Two

Letter Regarding the Oppenheimer Affair

From: Arthur Holly Compton
To: Gordan Gray, President of the UNC
Date: April 21, 1954

Park Hotel
Istanbul, Turkey
April 21, 1954

Dear President Gray:

I was in Pakistan when the news broke regarding the suspension of J. Robert Oppenheimer from the Advisory Board of the A. E. C., and it was not until yesterday that I received sufficiently full information about the case to make a statement that I knew would be relevant. Because of my close association with Oppenheimer, I believe that some facts from my first-hand knowledge will be useful to your committee in judging his loyalty. These facts I am stating here with the same responsibility for their veracity as I would accept in the case of sworn testimony before a court of law.

1. I was responsible for appointing Oppenheimer to the task of organizing whatever was necessary for designing the atomic bomb. This was about the end of April, 1942. (The dates given here are all approximate. I have here no notes regarding these matters, and all of my statements are from memory.) It was a month or two later that responsibility for the atomic development was assigned to the U. S. Engineers (Army), and it was

in September, 1942, that I recommended to General Groves that Oppenheimer be continued at this task, and that the responsibility be enlarged to include the construction of the bomb. This recommendation was in accord with that of others, in particular that of Dr. James Conant, and was accepted.

At the time of Oppenheimer's appointment the atomic development was, as you know, in civilian hands. By Dr. Conant, acting for the OSRD, I was given complete responsibility for such appointments, reporting to him, however, regarding actions taken. For my guidance, within our "Metallurgical Project," a personnel division had been established which investigated the loyalty background of employees. This investigation (and our other security measures) was carried on with the help of the Federal Bureau of Investigation. But we kept within our own hands the responsibility for the decisions in each case.

It was recognized that the task to which we were appointing Oppenheimer was not only of essential importance to the success of the total project, but also one in which a unique degree of discretion was required. It was my judgment that Oppenheimer's qualifications fitted him for such a post better than any other person who could be made available. This was after a diligent search for about a month which included consultation with many top-level scientists.

That Oppenheimer had had contacts with Communists was well known to me. These contacts, as I knew them, were essentially as described in his letter as published in The New York Times of April 13. It was my impression that, as one eager to find a solution to world problems, he had investigated Communism first-hand to see what it had to offer.

The much more significant fact was that he had already become disillusioned with Communism by what he had found. In a conversation with him about another matter, in the spring of 1940, I believe, he had given me his reasons for not associating himself with a professional organization that had some Communist

151

ties. Later, in 1941, I believe, he had told me of his efforts to persuade his brother Frank to dissociate himself from Communist groups. As I recall it, it was during the early stages of our conversations about the atomic program, before I had approached him about accepting the responsibility for the design of the bomb, that Oppenheimer told me he was breaking completely every association with any organization that might be suspected of Communism, in order that he might be of maximum usefulness on war projects.

It was my judgment that a person who had known Communism and had found its faults was more to be relied upon than one who was innocent of such connections. This was the more important because it was evident that his task would necessarily draw in many men of foreign background, who were among those most competent in theoretical physics. Without the use of such men his task could hardly have been accomplished. A man with Oppenheimer's experience both in foreign countries and, in a limited way, with Communism, was in a most favorable position to recognize those whose loyalties might be directed elsewhere than to the United States and the free world.

The chief positive reason for selecting Oppenheimer for this post was that after working vigorously on rallying the help of theoretical physicists to the design of the bomb, Oppenheimer had shown the most eagerness and initiative, he was one of the very few American-born men who had the professional competence, and he had demonstrated a certain firmness of character. While his administrative competence remained to be demonstrated, it looked to me promising.

Looking back on this selection, I do not believe it would have been possible to find anywhere a man better suited to carry through this unique job in the nation's interest.

2. After the war was over I discussed with Oppenheimer several times the question of proceeding with the development of the H-bomb. Its possibility Oppenheimer had called to my attention in August,

1942. This possibility was kept under the utmost secrecy; but before the war was over its suggestion had arisen spontaneously from so many sources that it was evident that it would arise in any group working seriously on nuclear explosions. In particular, it was evident that the basic principle of the fusion bomb would be known in Russia.

Immediately after the war our great consideration was to reach a reliable agreement with Russia that would rule out atomic weapons but permit the development of atomic power. During this period there was no immediate occasion to work toward atomic fusion. The situation changed when Russia showed such reluctance that no atomic weapon agreement seemed feasible. We then recognized that Russia was working vigorously on her own atomic development. Presumably the H-bomb would eventually become part of her program.

I recall a conversation with Oppenheimer in 1947 or 48 in which I was advocating the initiation of a program of active research and development toward the H-bomb. My point was that this development, if it was physically possible, was sure to come before many years, and it was important that the availability of this "super" weapon should first be in our hands.

I found Oppenheimer reluctant. His chief reluctance was, I believe, on purely moral grounds. No nation should bring into being a power that would (or could) be so destructive of human lives. Even if another nation should do so, our morality should be higher than this. We should accept the military disadvantage in the interest of standing for a proper moral principle.

He had other reasons – the development of fear and antagonism among other nations, the substantial possibility that the effort to create an atomic explosion would fail, questions regarding the H-bomb's military value. He hoped that no urgent need for its development would arise.

In this and other conversations Oppenheimer brought up precisely those questions that needed to be considered. His thinking seemed to be aimed solely toward finding what was in the best interests of the United States. He took for granted, as did L that the United States' interests are those of humanity. There was no shadow of a suspicion that his arguments were subtly working toward Russia's advantage. I am confident that no such thought was in his mind.

With the explosion of Russia's first atomic bomb in 1949 the situation was sharply changed. I do not recall any first-hand discussions with Oppenheimer on this matter after that date.

3. Having known Robert Oppenheimer since his days in Gottingen in 1927, having worked with him closely during the war years, and having kept in touch with him occasionally since, it is my judgment that he is completely loyal to the interests of the United States, and that any activity in the interest of a foreign power at the expense of the United States would be thoroughly repugnant to him. It is my judgment further that he is, and has been since 1941, just as thoroughly opposed to Communism.

Your sincerely,
Arthur H. Compton
AHC:dbs

(Permanent address,
Washington University,
St. Louis, MO. U.S.A.)

Oppenheimer's Letter of Response on Letter Regarding the Oppenheimer Affair

From: J R Oppenheimer
To: K.D. Nichols
Date: March 4, 1954

In the spring of 1936, I had been introduced by friends to Jean Tatlock, the daughter of a noted professor of English at the university; and in the autumn, I began to court her, and we grew close to each other. We were at least twice close enough to marriage to think of ourselves as engaged. Between 1939 and her death in 1944 I saw her very rarely. She told me about her Communist Party memberships; they were on again, off again affairs, and never seemed to provide for her what she was seeking. I do not believe that her interests were really political. She loved this country and its people and its life. She was, as it turned out, a friend of many fellow travelers and Communists, with a number of whom I was later to become acquainted.

I should not give the impression that it was wholly because of Jean Tatlock that I made left wing friends, or felt sympathy for causes which hitherto would have seemed so remote from me, like the Loyalist cause in Spain, and the organization of migratory workers. I have mentioned some of the other contributing causes. I liked the new sense of companionship, and at the time felt that I was coming to be part of the life of my time and country.

In 1937, my father died; a little later, when I came into an inheritance, I made a will leaving this to the University of California for fellowships to graduate students.

This was the era of what the Communists then called the United Front, in which they joined with many non-Communist groups in support of humanitarian objectives. Many of these objectives engaged my interest. I contributed to the strike fund of one of the major strikes of Bridges' union; I subscribed to the People's World; I contributed to the various committees and organizations which were intended to help the Spanish Loyalist cause. I was invited to help establish the teacher's union, which included faculty and teaching assistants at the university, and school teachers of the East Bay. I was elected recording secretary. My connection with the teacher's union continued until some time in 1941, when we disbanded our chapter....

My own views were also evolving. Although Sidney and Beatrice Webb's book on Russia, which I had read in 1936, and the talk that I heard at that time had predisposed me to make much of the economic progress and general level of welfare in Russia, and little of its political tyranny, my views on this were to change. I read about the purge trials, though not in full detail, and could never find a view of them which was not damning to the Soviet system. In 1938 1 met three physicists who had actually lived in Russia in the thirties. All were eminent scientists, Placzek, Weisskopf, and Schein; and the first two have become close friends. What they reported seemed to me so solid, so unfanatical, so true, that it made great impression; and it presented Russia, even when seen from their limited experience, as a land of purge and terror, of ludicrously bad management and of a long-suffering people. I need to make clear that this changing opinion of Russia, which was to be reinforced by the Nazi-Soviet Pact, and the behavior of the Soviet Union in Poland and in Finland, did not mean a sharp break for me with those who held to different views. At that time I did not fully understand – as in time I came to understand – how completely the Communist Party in this country was under the control of Russia. During and after the battle of France, however, and during the battle of England the next autumn, I found myself increasingly out of sympathy with the policy of disengagement and neutrality that the Communist press advocated. . .

Because of these associations that I have described, and the contributions mentioned earlier, I might well have appeared at the time as quite close to the Communist Party – perhaps even to some people as belonging to it. As I have said, some of its declared objectives seemed to me desirable. But I never was a member of the Communist Party. I never accepted Communist dogma or theory; in fact, it never made sense to me. I had no clearly formulated political views. I hated tyranny and repression and every form of dictatorial control of thought. In most cases I did not in those days know who was and who was not a member of the Communist Party. No one ever asked me to join the Communist Party....

In 1943 when I was alleged to have stated that I knew several individuals then at Los Alamos who had been members of the Communist Party," I knew of only one; she was my wife, of whose disassociation from the party, and of whose integrity and loyalty to the United States I had no question. Later, in 1944 or 1945, my brother Frank, who had been cleared for work in Berkeley and at Oak, Ridge, came to Los Alamos from Oak Ridge with official approval.

I knew of no attempt to obtain secret information at Los Alamos. Prior to my going there my friend Haakon Chevalier with his wife visited us on Eagle Hill, probably in early 1943. During the visit, he came into the kitchen and told me that George Eltenton had spoken to him of the possibility of transmitting technical information

THE SECRET OF THE THREE BULLETS

to Soviet scientists. I made some strong remark to the effect that this sounded terribly wrong to me. The discussion ended there. Nothing in our long standing friendship would have led me to believe that Chevalier was actually seeking information; and I was certain that he had no idea of the work on which I was engaged.

It has long been clear to me that I should have reported the incident at once. The events that led me to report it – which I doubt ever would have become known without my report – were unconnected with it. During the summer of 1943, Colonel Landsdale, the intelligence officer of the Manhattan District, came to Los Alamos and told me that he was worried about the security situation in Berkeley because of the activities of the Federation of Architects, Engineers, Chemists, and Technicians. This recalled to my mind that Eltenton was a member and probably a promoter of the FAECT. Shortly thereafter, I was in Berkeley and I told the security officer that Eltenton would bear watching(44). When asked why, I said that Eltenton had attempted, through intermediaries, to approach people on the project, though I mentioned neither myself nor Chevalier. Later, when General Groves urged me to give the details, I told him of my conversation with Chevalier. I still think of Chevalier as a friend....

From the close of the war, when I returned to the west coast until finally in the spring of 1947 when I went to Princeton as the director of the Institute for Advanced Study, I was able to spend very little time at home and in teaching in California. In October 1945, at the request of Secretary of War Patterson, I had testified before the House Committee on Military Affairs in support of the May-Johnson bill, which I endorsed as an interim means of bringing about without delay the much needed transition from the wartime administration of the Manhattan District to postwar management of the atomic-energy enterprise. In December 1945, and later, I appeared at Senator McMahoris request in sessions of his Special Committee on Atomic Energy, which was considering legislation on the same subject. Under the chairmanship of Dr. Richard Tolman, I served on a committee set up by General Groves to consider classification policy on matters of atomic energy. For 2 months, early in 1946, I worked steadily as a member of a panel, the Board of Consultants to the Secretary of State's Committee on Atomic Energy, which, with the Secretary of State's Committee, prepared the so-called Acheson-Lilienthal report. After the publication of this report, I spoke publicly in support of it. A little later, when Mr. Baruch was appointed to represent the United States in the United Nations Atomic Energy Committee, I became one of the scientific consultants to Mr. Baruch, and his staff in preparation for and in the conduct of our efforts to gain support for the United States' plan. I continued as a consultant to General Osborn when he took over the effort.

At the end of 1946 1 was appointed by the President as a member of the General Advisory Committee to the Atomic Energy Commission. At its first meeting I was elected Chairman, and was reelected until the expiration of my term in 1952. This was my principal assignment during these years as far as the atomic-energy program was concerned, and my principal preoccupation apart from academic work....

The initial members of the General Advisory Committee were Conant, then president of Harvard, DuBridge, president of the California Institute of Technology, Fermi of the University of Chicago, Rabi of Columbia University, Rowe, vice president of the United Fruit Co., Seaborg of the University of California, Cyril Smith of the University of Chicago, and Worthington of the duPont Co. In 1948 Buckley, president of the Bell Telephone Laboratories, replaced Worthington; in the summer of 1950, Fermi, Rowe, and Seaborg were replaced by Libby of the University of Chicago, Murphree president of Standard Oil Development Co., and Whitman of the Massachusetts Institute of Technology. Later Smith resigned and was succeeded by von Neumann of the Institute for Advanced Study.

In these years from early 1947 to mid-1952 the Committee met some 30 times and transmitted perhaps as many reports to the Commission. Formulation of policy and the management of the vast atomic-energy enterprises were responsibilities vested in the Commission itself. The General Advisory Committee had the role, which was fixed for it by statute, to advise the Commission. In that capacity we gave the Commission our views on questions which the Commission put before us, brought to the Commissions' attention on our initiative technical matters of importance, and encouraged and supported the work of the several major installations of the Commission....

The super itself had a long history of consideration beginning, as I have said, with our initial studies in 1942 before Los Alamos was established, it continued to be the subject of study and research at Los Alamos throughout the war. After the war, Los Alamos itself was inevitably handicapped pending the enactment of necessary legislation for the atomic energy enterprise. With the McMahon Act, the appointment of the Atomic Energy Commission and the General Advisory Committee, we in the committee had occasion at our early meetings in 1947 as well as in 1948 to discuss the subject. In that period the General Advisory Committee pointed out the still extremely unclear status of the problem from the technical standpoint, and urged encouragement of Los Alamos' efforts which were then directed toward modest exploration of the super and of thermonuclear systems. No serious controversy arose about the super until the Soviet explosion of an atomic bomb in the autumn of 1949.

Shortly after that event, in October 1949, the Atomic Energy Commission called a special session of the General Advisory Committee and asked us to consider and advise on two related questions: First, whether in view of the Soviet success the Commission's program was adequate, and if not, in what way it should be altered or increased; second, whether a crash program for the development of the super should be a part of any new program. The committee considered both questions, consulting various officials from the civil and military branches of the executive departments who would have been concerned, and reached conclusions which were communicated in a report to the Atomic Energy Commission in October 1949.

This report, in response to the first question that had been put to us, recommended a great number of measures that the Commission should take to increase in many ways our overall potential in weapons.

As to the super itself, the General Advisory Committee stated its unanimous opposition to the initiation by the United States of a crash program of the kind we had been asked to advise on. The report of that meeting, and the Secretary's notes, reflect the reasons which moved us to this conclusion. The annexes, in particular, which dealt more with political and policy considerations – the report proper was essentially technical in character indicated differences in the views of members of the committee. There were two annexes, one signed by Rabi and Fermi, the other by Conant, DuBridge, Smith, Rowe, Buckley and myself. (The ninth member of the committee, Seaborg, was abroad at the time.)

It would have been surprising if eight men considering a problem of extreme difficulty had each had precisely the same reasons for the conclusion in which we joined. But I think I am correct in asserting that the unanimous opposition we expressed to the crash program was based on the conviction, to which technical considerations as well as others contributed, that because of our overall situation at that time such a program might weaken rather than strengthen the position of the United States.

After the report was submitted to the Commission, it fell to me as chairman of the committee to explain our position on several occasions, once at a meeting of the joint Congressional Committee on Atomic Energy. All this, however, took place prior to the decision by the President to proceed with the thermonuclear program.

This is the full story of my "opposition to the hydrogen bomb." It can be read in the records of the general transcript of my testimony before the joint congressional committee. It is a story which ended once and for all when in January 1950 the President announced his decision to proceed with the program. I never urged anyone not to work on the hydrogen bomb project. I never made or caused any distribution of the GAC reports except to the Commission itself. As always, it was the Commission's responsibility to determine further distribution.

In summary, in October 1949, I and the other members of the General Advisory Committee were asked questions by the Commission to which we had a duty to respond, and to which we did respond with our best judgment in the light of evidence then available to us....

In this letter, I have written only of those limited parts of my history which appear relevant to the issue now before the Atomic Energy Commission. In order to preserve as much as possible the perspective of the story, I have dealt very briefly with many matters. I have had to deal briefly or not at all with instances in which my actions or views were adverse to Soviet or Communist interest, and of actions that testify to my devotion to freedom, or that have contributed to the vitality, influence and power of the United States.

In preparing this letter, I have reviewed two decades of my life. I have recalled instances where I acted unwisely. What I have hoped was, not that I could wholly avoid error, but that I might learn from it. What I have learned has, I think, made me more fit to serve my country.

Very truly yours,
J. Robert Oppenheimer
Princeton, N.J., March 4, 1954

Appendix Four

THE RUSSELL-EINSTEIN
MANIFESTO

Issued in London, 9 July 1955

I n the tragic situation which confronts humanity, we feel
that scientists should assemble in conference to appraise
the perils that have arisen as a result of the development
of weapons of mass destruction, and to discuss a resolution
in the spirit of the appended draft.

We are speaking on this occasion, not as members of
this or that nation, continent, or creed, but as human beings, members of the species Man, whose continued existence is in doubt. The world is full of conflicts; and, over-
shadowing all minor conflicts, the titanic struggle between
Communism and anti-Communism.

Almost everybody who is politically conscious has
strong feelings about one or more of these issues; but we
want you, if you can, to set aside such feelings and consider
yourselves only as members of a biological species which
has had a remarkable history, and whose disappearance
none of us can desire.

We shall try to say no single word which should appeal
to one group rather than to another. All, equally, are in peril,
and, if the peril is understood, there is hope that they may
collectively avert it.

We have to learn to think in a new way. We have to learn
to ask ourselves, not what steps can be taken to give military

victory to whatever group we prefer, for there no longer are such steps; the question we have to ask ourselves is: what steps can be taken to prevent a military contest of which the issue must be disastrous to all parties?

The general public, and even many men in positions of authority, have not realized what would be involved in a war with nuclear bombs. The general public still thinks in terms of the obliteration of cities. It is understood that the new bombs are more powerful than the old, and that, while one A-bomb could obliterate Hiroshima, one H-bomb could obliterate the largest cities, such as London, New York, and Moscow.

No doubt in an H-bomb war great cities would be obliterated. But this is one of the minor disasters that would have to be faced. If everybody in London, New York, and Moscow were exterminated, the world might, in the course of a few centuries, recover from the blow. But we now know, especially since the Bikini test, that nuclear bombs can gradually spread destruction over a very much wider area than had been supposed.

It is stated on very good authority that a bomb can now be manufactured which will be 2,500 times as powerful as that which destroyed Hiroshima. Such a bomb, if exploded near the ground or under water, sends radioactive particles into the upper air. They sink gradually and reach the surface of the earth in the form of a deadly dust or rain. It was this dust which infected the Japanese fishermen and their catch of fish.

No one knows how widely such lethal radioactive particles might be diffused, but the best authorities are unanimous in saying that a war with H-bombs might possibly put an end to the human race. It is feared that if many H-bombs are used there will be universal death, sudden only for a minority, but for the majority a slow torture of disease and disintegration.

Many warnings have been uttered by eminent men of science and by authorities in military strategy. None of them will say that the worst results are certain. What they do say is that these results are possible, and no one can be sure that they will not be realized. We have not yet found that the views of experts on this question depend in any degree upon their politics or prejudices. They depend only, so far as our researches have revealed, upon the extent of the particular expert's knowledge. We have found that the men who know most are the most gloomy.

Here, then, is the problem which we present to you, stark and dreadful and inescapable: Shall we put an end to the human race; or shall mankind renounce war? People will not face this alternative because it is so difficult to abolish war.

The abolition of war will demand distasteful limitations of national sovereignty. But what perhaps impedes understanding of the situation more than anything else is that the term "mankind" feels vague and abstract. People scarcely realize in imagination that the danger is to themselves and their children and their grandchildren, and not only to a dimly apprehended humanity. They can scarcely bring themselves to grasp that they, individually, and those whom they love are in imminent danger of perishing agonizingly. And so they hope that perhaps war may be allowed to continue provided modern weapons are prohibited.

This hope is illusory. Whatever agreements not to use H-bombs had been reached in time of peace, they would no longer be considered binding in time of war, and both sides would set to work to manufacture H-bombs as soon as war broke out, for, if one side manufactured the bombs and the other did not, the side that manufactured them would inevitably be victorious.

Although an agreement to renounce nuclear weapons as part of a general reduction of armaments would not afford an ultimate solution, it would serve certain important purposes. First: any agreement between East and West is to the good in so far as it tends to diminish tension. Second: the abolition of thermonuclear weapons, if each side believed that the other had carried it out sincerely, would lessen the fear of a sudden attack in the style of Pearl Harbor, which at present keeps both sides in a state of nervous apprehension. We should, therefore, welcome such an agreement though only as a first step. Most of us are not neutral in feeling, but, as human beings, we have to remember that, if the issues between East and West are to be decided in any manner that can give any possible satisfaction to anybody, whether Communist or anti-Communist, whether Asian or European or American, whether White or Black, then these issues must not be decided by war. We should wish this to be understood, both in the East and in the West. There lies before us, if we choose, continual progress in happiness, knowledge, and wisdom. Shall we, instead, choose death, because we cannot forget our quarrels? We appeal, as human beings, to human beings: Remember your humanity, and forget the rest. If you can do so, the way lies open to a new Paradise; if you cannot, there lies before you the risk of universal death.

Resolution

We invite this Congress, and through it the scientists of the world and the general public, to subscribe to the following resolution:

"In view of the fact that in any future world war nuclear weapons will certainly be employed, and that such weapons threaten the continued existence of mankind, we urge the Governments of the world to realize, and to acknowledge publicly, that their purpose cannot be furthered by a world war, and we urge them, consequently, to find peaceful means for the settlement of all matters of dispute between them."

Max Born
Perry W. Bridgman
Albert Einstein
Leopold Infeld
Frederic Joliot-Curie
Herman J. Muller
Linus Pauling
Cecil F. Powell
Joseph Rotblat
Bertrand Russell
Hideki Yukawa

Appendix Five

GLOVE MEMORANDUM

Memorandum to:
Brigadier General L. R. Groves
Drs. Conant, Compton, and Urey
War Department
United States Engineer Office
Manhattan District
Oak Ridge Tennessee
October 30, 1943
Declassified June 5, 1974

1. Inclosed [sic] is a summary of the report written by Drs. James B. Conant, Chairman, A. H. Compton, and H. C. Urey, comprising a Subcommittee of the S-1 Executive Committee on the "Use of Radioactive Materials as a Military Weapon." It is recommended that a decision be obtained from competent authority authorizing additional work pertaining to the use of radioactive materials in order that this country may be ready to use such materials or be ready to defend itself against the use of such materials. The following program is recommended:

   a. Immediate formation of a research and study group at the University of Chicago under supervision of the present Area Engineer. Assignment to this group of competent individuals now working on dust and liquid disseminating munitions and field testing of chemical warfare agents from the National Defense Research Council.

   b. Assignment of a competent Chemical Warfare Service officer to the Chicago Area Engineer, who would become familiar with, and work on the problem under study by the University of Chicago. This officer should be experienced in the practical use of gas warfare.

c. The responsibility of the above organization would be:

(1) Develop radiation indicating instruments, expand present facilities of the Victoreen Company, and prepare a trial order for instruments with this company.

(2) Make theoretical studies pertaining to the methods, means and equipment for disseminating radioactive material as a weapon of warfare.

(3) Conduct field tests in isolated locations, such as Clinton Engineer Works or Sanford Engineer Works, using a non-radioactive tracer material.

(4) Prepare an instruction manual for the use of, or the defense against, radioactive weapons. This manual would be similar to that now used by the Chemical Warfare Service for gas warfare.

(2) <u>As a gas warfare instrument</u> the material would be ground into particles of microscopic size to form dust and smoke and distributed by a ground-fired projectile, land vehicles, or aerial bombs. In this form it would be inhaled by personnel. The amount necessary to cause death to a person inhaling the material is extremely small. It has been estimated that one millionth of a gram accumulating in a person's body would be fatal. There are no known methods of treatment for such a casualty

Two factors appear to increase the effectiveness of radioactive dust or smoke as a weapon. These are: (1) It cannot be detected by the senses; (2) It can be distributed in a dust or smoke form so finely powdered that it will permeate a standard gas mask filter in quantities large enough to be extremely damaging. An off-setting factor in its effectiveness as a weapon is that in a dust or smoke form the material is so finely pulverized that it takes on the characteristic of a quickly dissipating gas and is therefore subject to all the factors (such as wind) working against maintenance of high concentrations for more than a few minutes over a given area.

c. <u>Possible Use by the Enemy</u>.

It is felt that radioactive warfare can be used by the Germans for the following purposes:

(1) To make evacuated areas uninhabitable.

(2) To contaminate small critical areas such as railroad yards and airports.

(3) As a radioactive poison gas to create casualties among troops.

(4) Against large cities, to promote panic, and create causalities among civilian populations.

For use in cities, it is estimated that concentrations would have to be extremely high to offset the shielding effect of buildings

Doctors Compton and Urey, two members of the Committee, felt that radioactive material may be used by the Germans against United Nations in the autumn of 1943. Dr. Conant apparently does not concur in this opinion.

d. <u>Possible Use by the United States</u>.

It is the recommendation of this Subcommittee that if military authorities feel that the United States should be ready to use radioactive weapons in case the enemy started it first, studies on the subject should be started immediately.

The possible military uses of radioactive materials follow:

(1) As a Terrain Contaminant. To be used in this manner, the radioactive materials would be spread on the ground either from the air or from the ground if in enemy controlled territory. In order to deny terrain to either side except at the expense of exposing personnel to harmful radiations

Estimates indicate that these materials could be produced by the Germans in such quantities that each four days two square miles of terrain could be contaminated to an average intensity of radiation three feet above ground level of one hundred roentgens per day. One day's exposure (100 roentgens to the whole body) would result in temporary incapacitation, a lesser period of exposure in incapacitation to a lesser degree and one week's exposure in death. Effects on a person would probably not be immediate, but would be delayed for days or perhaps weeks depending upon the amounts of exposure. Exposure to five to ten times the above described concentration would be incapacitating within one to two days and lethal two to five days later.

Areas so contaminated by radioactive material would be dangerous until the slow natural decay of the material took place, which would take weeks and even months. On a hard smooth surface some decontamination could be accomplished by flushing with water, but for average terrain no decontaminating methods are known. No effective protective clothing for personnel seems possible of development.

(2) As a Gas Warfare Instrument. The material would be ground into particles of microscopic size and would be distributed in the form of a dust or smoke or dissolved in liquid, by ground-fired projectiles, land vehicles, airplanes, or aerial bombs. In this form, it would be inhaled by personnel. The amounts necessary to cause death to a person inhaling the material is extremely small. An infinitesimal amount accumulating in a person's body would be fatal in a few day to weeks depending upon the amount absorbed and its radioactivity. There are no known effective methods of treatment for such a casualty.

Areas so contaminated by radioactive dusts and smokes, would be dangerous as long as a high enough concentration of material could be maintained. In these forms, the materials take on the characteristics of a quickly dissipating gas and it is improbable that heavy concentrations could be maintained for more than a few minutes time over a given area. However, they can be stirred up as a fine dust from the terrain by winds, movement of vehicles or troops, etc. , and would remain a potential hazard for a long time.

These materials may also be so disposed as to be taken into the body by ingestion instead of inhalation.. Reservoirs or wells would be contaminated or food poisoned with an effect similar to that resulting from inhalation of dust or smoke. Four days production could contaminate a million gallons of water to an extent that a quart drunk in one day would probably result in complete incapacitation or death in about a month's time.

– PAGE 2 –

B. From Internal Sources

RESPIRATORY TRACT: Dr. Wollan has estimated that an accumulation of 10^{-3} curies of high-energy beta-ray active material would produce an exposure of about 100 r/day to the lungs. Unfortunately, there is no experimental data bearing directly upon the deposition off products nor on the action of the beta-rays on the bronchial and alveolar surfaces.

Particles larger than 1μ[micron]in size are likely to be deposited in nose, trachea or bronchi and then be brought up with mucus on the walls at the rate of 1/2 – 1 cm/min. Particles smaller than 1μ [micron] are more likely to be deposited in the alveoli where they will either remain indefinitely or be absorbed into the lymphatics or blood. The probability of the deposition of dust particles anywhere in the respiratory tract depends upon respiratory rate, particle size, chemical and physical nature, and the concentration in the atmosphere. Hence the probability off products causing lung damage depends on all of these factors.

While only fragmentary information is available, it is felt that the injury would be manifest as bronchial irritation coming on in from a few hours to a few days, depending on the dose. It would not be immediately incapacitating except with doses in the neighborhood of 400 or more r [roentgens] per day. The most serious effect would be permanent long damage appearing months later from the persistent irradiation of retained particles, even at low daily rates.

It would seem that chemical gases could accomplish more and do it more quickly so far as the skin surfaces and lungs are concerned. The beta emitters would have more permanent effects – starting months after exposure.

GASTRO-INTESTINAL TRACT: Beta emitting f [fission] products could get into the gastro-intestinal tract from polluted water, or food, or air. From the air, they would get onto the mucus of the nose, throat, bronchi, etc., and be swallowed. The effects would be local irritation just as in the bronchi and exposures of the same amount would be required. The stomach, caecum, and rectum, where contents remain for longer periods than elsewhere would be most likely to be affected. It is conceivable that ulcers and perforations of the gut followed by death could be produced, even without any general effects from the radiation.

BLOOD STREAM AND TISSUES: Beta and gamma emitting fission products may be absorbed from the lungs or G-I tract into the blood and so distributed throughout the body.

This document contains information affecting the national defense of the United States within the meaning of the Espionage Act, U.S.C. 50: 31 and 32. Its transmission or the revelation of its contents in any manner to an unauthorized person is prohibited by law.

NOTES

1. The National Research Defense Council was the body which had the task of "directing" scientific research for the Pentagon.

2. *Dr. Strangelove or: 'How I Learned to Stop Worrying and Love the Bomb,'* filmed in 1964 by Stanley Kubrick and loosely based on the novel 'Red Alert' by Peter George. The main actor is Peter Sellers who plays three different characters.

3. During hot fusion of two deuterium nuclei, the following product results are obtained: a) in 50% of cases: neutron + helium-3; b) in the remaining 50%: proton + tritium; c) there is a third, extremely rare case, about one in a million, when helium 4 + gamma rays are obtained. Whereas, the cold fusion of two deuterium nuclei produces, in almost all cases, helium 4 + heat.

4. The CEA High Commissioner, René Pellat, who met with the ENEA group, died two weeks later while swimming off the coast of Brittany.

5. Regarding this issue, one should read the three letters on the Oppenheimer case published at the end of the novel.

6. G. Herken, *Brotherhood of the Bomb: The tangled lives and loyalties of Robert Oppenheimer, Ernest Lawrence and Edward Teller* (Henry Holt, New York 2002: Fermi on p. 25, Ulam on p. 137).

7. Stix, Gary (October 1999). 'Infamy and honor at the Atomic Café: Edward Teller has no regrets about his contentious career', *Scientific American*: 42-43.

8. From the transcription of the Oppenheimer case, U.S. Atomic Energy Commission.

9. 'The Work of Many People', published in *Science Magazine* in February 1955.

10. Stix, Gary (October 1999). 'Infamy and honor at the Atomic Café: Edward Teller has no regrets about his contentious career'. Scientific American: 42-43.

11. 'Project Chariot'

12. By extension, one could analyze how ceramic materials can accommodate hydrogen.

13. An electrically charged molecule or atom is defined as an ion because it has lost or gained one or more electrons than a neutral atom. Ionization usually occurs by applying high energy to the atoms, in the form of electric potential or radiation.

14. Imagine the atom as consisting of three types of spheres. The red ones, negatively charged, are electrons that revolve around the nucleus, which contains two different types of spheres: positively charged black ones (protons), and electrically neutral gray ones (neutrons). An isotope is an atom of a given chemical element, with the same number of black and red spheres, protons and electrons (atomic number), but with a different number of gray spheres (neutrons), thus with a different mass number. Some isotopes are radioactive, i.e. unstable, even though they often have an extremely long decay lifetime.

15. LENR, Low Energy Nuclear Reaction.

16. Whose molecules consist of an oxygen atom and 2 atoms of deuterium, an isotope of hydrogen whose nucleus consists of a proton and a neutron. It is called "heavy water" precisely because of these two extra neutrons.

17. The process was helped by particular particles similar to electrons, muons.

18. The scientist who had previously worked at length on the "Star wars" project proposed by Ronald Reagan.

19. In synthesis, the cold fusion process was as follows: by using electrolysis, an amount of deuterium, much greater than the quantity usually taken into consideration by electrochemists, was placed inside the palladium. After charging for at least four weeks, abnormal amounts of energy appeared that were compatible with a nuclear process and inconsistent with a chemical process. In fact, the energy produced was in the order of hundreds of electron volts per atom of palladium, whereas the usual chemical processes produce not more than several dozen electron volts.

20. Hot fusion nuclear processes imply that the following possibilities eventually occur: 1) presence of a tritium nucleus (consisting of one proton and 2 neutrons) and a proton, 2) presence of a helium- 3 nucleus (consisting of 2 protons and one neutron) and a neutron, 3) presence of a gamma photon, with the probability of one in a million. However, the measurements reported by Fleischmann and Pons revealed the presence of neutrons or tritium or gamma photons in infinitesimal quantities compared to a process similar to that of hot fusion. In their article published in the Journal of Electroanalytical Chemistry, these same authors then claimed that the process they had discovered used a profoundly different method from hot fusion, so the final product of the reaction, apart from the energy, could only be helium 4 (2 protons and 2 neutrons), which they were not however able to measure because they lacked the necessary instruments. They therefore claimed that the measurements of the final reaction products that they had reported indicated that these products, which were only present in trace amounts, were not in anyway the main product of the reaction. Whereas the criticism that their experiments raised focused on the questionability of the presence of precisely those reaction products, surmising that Fleischmann and Pons had considered them to be proof of the nuclear nature of the process.

21. Finding the loading threshold at 95% of the presence of deuterium in palladium.

22. In 1991, Eugene Mallove, scientific editor in the MIT press office, realized that the report put out by the MIT Plasma Science and Fusion Center in 1989, in which the data on cold fusion were illustrated, had some graphs whose axes

had been deliberately moved so as to alter the results. Yet it was by no means a publication of little consequence, and in fact played an important role in the denigration of cold fusion. Mallove was convinced that there was great interest in denigrating cold fusion, because it could have diverted funding away from many of the great university research centers who were at that time doing research on hot fusion.

23. In 1992, experiments were carried out with palladium-boron alloys, all of which were successful.

24. Following a request by several academics and researchers who showed the positive results, during the International Conference on Cold Fusion, held in Boston in August 2003.

25. A final report was drawn up entitled "New Physical Effects in Metal Deuterides."

26. He graduated in aeronautical engineering at MIT and environmental science at Harvard, then worked for Hughes Research Laboratories, for the Analytich Science Corporation and for MIT itself.

27. Author of the book 'Fire from Ice: Searching for the Truth Behind the Cold Fusion Furor', he was very active, both as a science journalist – he wrote regularly for *Infinite Energy*, for example – and as an expert (he was frequently interviewed by the American program *Coast to Coast*.) He was also the consultant for the screenplay of the movie 'The Saint', a film in whose script reference was also made to some cold fusion formulas.

28. Professor René Pellat, Director of the National Center for Space Studies in France, and High Commissioner of the French Atomic Energy Commission, died from heart problems while swimming near Royan on August 4, 2003.

29. *Desert News* on March 25.

30. The parliamentary commission investigating depleted uranium decided to detonate 200 kg of high potential bombs, packed with depleted uranium and tungsten, in a so-called "stove" in Nasiriyah, Iraq, to study the chemical elements present after the explosion. According to the final report, the commission found dust with a chemical composition that was 'new' compared to the existing material in the stove, but added in the report "dependent on the material existing at the point of explosion." It was not a particularly successful paraphrase to assert that these were elements of fission material that had previously existed. They also found strontium, an element stemming from uranium fission.

31. Hague Convention on the Prohibition of the Use in War of Asphyxiating *Gas* July 29, 1899, not signed by the United States.

32. See text of the Russell-Einstein Manifesto to the rulers of the world, reported at the end of the book in the Materials section

33. 'Uranium appauvri, la guerre invisible' Edition Robert Laffont, Paris, (Depleted Uranium: The Invisible War), written by three journalists: Martin Meissonnier (French), Frederic Loore (Swiss) and Roger Trilling (American).

34 X.Z. Li, Y. J. Yan, J. Tian, M.Y. Mei, Y. Deng, W. Z. Yu, G. Y. Tang, D. X. Cao, A. De Ninno: 'Nuclear Transmutations in Pd deuteride', published on pages 123-

128 in the Proceedings of the 8th Annual Conference on Cold Fusion, edited in 2001 by the Italian Physical Society.

35. With this slang expression, Prof. Fleischmann presumably means a phenomenon consisting of the sequence of two processes, in which the first is the trigger for the second: for example, fission and fusion.

36. The research company in Europe was called Technova, and later renamed IMRA-EUROPE.

37. Toroidal magnetic chamber, a thermonuclear fusion power device.

38. See http://en.wikipedia.org/wiki/Richter_magnitude_scale

39. Read, in particular, the article by Voeikov published in the September to December 2009 issue of the Italian journal *La Medicina Biologica*.

40. The riddle, reasonably well known, was analyzed by Jacques Lacan in his essay 'Logical time and the assertion of anticipated certainty' (in the collection, Writings), which is however more simply explained by Kurt Grass.

41. Report on the findings of the investigations conducted by the Commission. Speaker: Senator Paolo Franco. Approved in the session held on 1 March 2006.

42. "It can be concluded that during the explosion of high potential bombs like those packed with depleted uranium or tungsten, or a group of bombs, a higher or lower temperature is triggered and dust may be created – with a 'new' chemical composition dependent on the material existing at the point of explosion – which may even be of nanometric size." P. 23

43. *Time* magazine online, Laura Fitzpatrick. 'In May, an unusual shipment made its way from Kuwait to Idaho: 6,700 tons of radioactive sand. The cargo, contaminated by traces of depleted uranium from military vehicles and munitions that caught on fire during the first Gulf War, was extracted from a U.S. army base and dumped at a hazardous waste disposal site 70 miles southeast of Boise. And this isn't the first shipment, either: in years past, the dump operator, American Ecology Corp., has ferried hazardous materials from U.S. military bases overseas to sites in Idaho, Nevada, and Texas. "As you can imagine," a company spokesman explained to the Associated Press, apparently without irony, "the host countries of those bases don't want the waste in their country."

44. The form used is "bear watching." Conventional expression for 'spying